Now a
Harle...
roma...
by Anne Mather
comes to life
on the movie screen

starring

KEIR DULLEA · SUSAN PENHALIGON

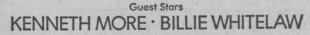

Leopard
in the
Snow

Guest Stars
KENNETH MORE · BILLIE WHITELAW

featuring GORDON THOMSON as MICHAEL
and JEREMY KEMP as BOLT

Produced by JOHN QUESTED and CHRIS HARROP
Screenplay by ANNE MATHER and JILL HYEM
Directed by GERRY O'HARA

An Anglo-Canadian Co-Production

OTHER
Harlequin Romances
by JOYCE DINGWELL

A Drift of Jasmine

by

JOYCE DINGWELL

Harlequin Books

TORONTO • LONDON • NEW YORK • AMSTERDAM • SYDNEY

Original hardcover edition published in 1977
by Mills & Boon Limited

ISBN 0-373-02123-2

Harlequin edition published December 1977

PRINTED IN U.S.A.

CHAPTER ONE

It was high noon by the time the safari coach to the Northern Territory pulled in at the unbelievably small outpost of Far-Flung.

The safari had left the Bitumen half an hour ago, and would take another thirty minutes to regain it, but Junia had paid for the detour, and none of her fellow passengers, whom she was saying goodbye to now, had seemed to mind. They were, they had reminded Junia, on holiday, so were only seeing more for their money. They were pleased about that, but not so pleased about Far-Flung for Junia, with whom, the way it is on vacation, they had become very friendly by now. In fact they even looked at the place with unconcealed dismay ... and then at Junia with pity. Meanwhile Junia, too busy waving and promising she would keep in touch, did not look at it at all until the cloud of red dust as the bus took off again at last subsided. Then she did turn and look. And gasped.

Far-Flung, she gulped, if nothing else was aptly named. As far as she could see there was space, and across that space was flung one filling station with one solitary pump, one windmill, one shack, one surprised gas attendant with one yellow dog, obviously his domesticated dingo, and that was all.

Still, she was at journey's end ... or at least getting near to it ... and that was something the tourist agent had tried to discourage.

'Yes, I am aware there is a prospecting project at Far-

Off' ... evidently someone up there, frustrated by distances, had prefaced these particular north-west places with Far ... 'but the staff always fly in by the company aircraft.'

'Perhaps I could, too,' Junia had suggested hopefully.

'I wouldn't know about that, we only overland, and we don't touch Far-Off, nor Far-Flung either for that matter, but Far-Flung wouldn't be so distant from our scheduled route.'

'That's what I hoped for,' Junia had nodded. 'According to my map I can make it myself from there. Do you think your firm could——'

'Yes, but you realise you would have to pay for the detour, and that after you left the coach at Far-Flung our responsibility would be ended?'

'I realise,' Junia had agreed, and had opened her purse.

The tourist agent, mollified, had warned: 'It's strictly a camping trip, you know, no hotels, no luxury.'

'That will suit me fine. It could prepare me for any privations that could lay ahead, though inland projects these days are made very comfortable, I believe—air-conditioning, good social life, the lot.' Junia had started counting out notes.

She had received a receipt and a memo on what and what not to take. If she didn't have camping gear, she could hire it on the coach.

'Great,' she had said, and had thanked the still faintly dubious agent and departed.

A few days later she had left Sydney, a week later again, a magic week of sunlit plains, of unbelievable desert nights beneath the stars, of campfires and sizzling steaks and good company, she had arrived here at Far-Flung, nearest stop to Far-Off, and had just now been rather soberly taken leave of, the soberness no

6

doubt because of *where* she had alighted, in which case Junia looked around her again, looked more closely, looked at the filling station, the windmill, the shack, the man and the dog. Particularly the man.

'Ned,' the man said, and he came forward and put out a big rough hand.

'Junia,' Junia responded, and took the hand.

They both shook hands, then Ned drawled: 'Reckon you haven't come to visit me, Junie' ... (because her name was unusual, Junia accepted that) ... 'seeing nobody has visited me ever since I came here, and that's over twenty years. So what?' He was rolling a cigarette.

'I want to get to Far-Off,' Junia confided, 'and according to my map——'

'According to your map it's only fifty miles away ... they tell me they're using something called kilos now, is that right? ... but fifty miles isn't correct any more.'

'Not correct?'

'Not since the Big Wet. No, it's much further these days.'

'Oh——' said Junia, and looked around her again.

When she had learned from the coach driver that Far-Flung was a filling station it had seemed to her that her troubles were over. She would simply hire a car from the garage and be over at Far-Off in no time, then once there she would have Colin return the car to its owner. But apart from a bowser and rough office, Junia could see nothing else. Certainly she could see no car, for private use or hire. Anyway, according to this Ned, it was no longer a mere fifty-mile hop, not since something called a Big Wet.

Ned was telling her about the Big Wet now. Never had they had such a wet before, he said. The Lucy River had reached seventy miles across and what had

7

once been dry desert had blossomed. Flowers every-where.

It was levelling out now, Ned went on, but there was still a lot of left-over water, and that was why Far-Off was now much further away than before. You had long hazardous detours.

'Sure you have to go?' he finished persuasively. 'I could do with a pump hand.'

'It certainly seems like it,' laughed Junia. 'No, I have to go, Ned. It's not forbidden, by any chance, is it?' That had occurred to her several times as a reason for Colin's neglecting to ask her up here definitely. Oh, he had said: 'Some time' ... 'Later' ... 'If you come——' but never made a firm arrangement. Lots of projects, she knew, were out of bounds while secrets were being unearthed, so perhaps Far-Off——

'No, Far-Off is still open to fools and kangaroos,' Ned said cheerfully.

'You think the men are fools?'

'Anyone who digs holes is a fool,' shrugged Ned. 'No, you're jake, girl. No restriction. The only trouble is getting there.'

'No car, Ned?' she queried.

'No car, Junie.'

'Do any of the Far-Off craft land around here?'

'No, there's a proper strip at Far-Away.'—Another Far!—'Your only hope is a chance motorist ... or the supply truck. The supply comes in once a week to pick up the necessaries that are left by the road train, and, believe your luck or not, today's the day.'

'Beaut,' appreciated Junia with relief. 'Do you think——'

'With Karl Kemble, Junie, you don't think, you just take him as he comes.'

'Is he the driver?'

8

'He's the boss of so much of Far-Off that what's left over doesn't matter.'

'But a boss wouldn't drive, surely, so perhaps his driver——'

'But Karl does drive. He brings a boy for relief, but he still drives—the same as he still digs, still puts down pegs, still gelignites an outcrop, still writes reports, still analyses. Oh, he just doesn't run the show, he *is* the show.'

'I see,' said Junia. She was thoughtful for a long moment. 'And you have to take him as he comes?' she asked carefully.

'Exactly. Good mood, bad mood—who knows? Well, can you blame him? He has a heck of responsibility.'

'But a boss can still be reasonable.'

'With reasonable people. He's had a bit of trouble lately.'

'Trouble?'

'Usual hole-in-the-ground worries, if you follow me.'

Junia did not, but she did not admit it.

'And you think he might consider me more trouble?' she smiled at Ned.

He grinned back at her, obviously won over. 'I reckon you wouldn't trouble anyone. I reckon if you look like that at Karl, you'll be sure of a hitch, and I'll be short of my bowser girl. See that blob of dust?' Ned pointed to a distant roseate cloud. 'That'll be the supply truck. I'll push off home for a few chores I hadn't finished doing when your safari crowd pulled in. If you're still here when I come back again, Junie, you're as good as signed on, but if you've wangled yourself that hitch, then good luck to you, kid.' He grinned at Junia, then loped off in the direction of his hut, his yellow dog beside him.

'Give K.K. my regards,' he called as he went.

After he had gone Junia took out her compact and did all she could to her face. She had plenty of time, for the supply truck was still a distant blob of dust. She combed her long brown hair and tied it back with a red ribbon, put on a new mouth. Ned had advised her to smile her best, and if it could get her to Far-Off ... and Colin ... she must use every wile.

She sat down on her pack when she had done and watched the cloud come closer. It was scarcely the way, she thought a little wryly, making patterns in the dust with the toe of her shoe, that she had expected to join Colin. Certainly a hitch in a supply truck had never entered her mind.

When Colin had resigned from the Sydney office, where she, too, worked, some six months ago to go 'bush', as he called it, none of his friends ... nor Junia ... had expected him to last very long. He was not outback-minded. He was also, and fondly but honestly Junia had to admit it, not the stay-put type. Since she had known him he had been in and out of jobs so frequently she had been unable to keep up with them. Which made her very proud of him now that Colin had stuck it out up here. If only he had sent for her, sent for her *definitely*, not just written: 'Some time' ... 'Later' ... 'If you come——' everything would have been perfect.

But now instead she was coming to him ... well, you did that for someone you loved ... and though Junia knew that she should have told him, she knew, too, that with one look at each other everything would be all right.

I *know* it, she told the red dust.

The blob was coming closer now, you could tell its shape. It was a very large table-top truck with a high canvas canopy. Ned had spoken of supplies. Junia looked back at the shed and saw stacks of containers and cartons arrayed along the wall evidently waiting to be picked up. Well, Mr Karl Kemble ... she thought that was the name ... something else was waiting to be picked up. A some*body*. She checked her face again.

Now the truck was clearly visible. An aboriginal boy was driving it. Beside the boy sat a man, a large man by the head and shoulders advantage on the driver, and with a shock of hair that fascinated Junia. Part of it was red from the red dust, part of it grey from the pall thrown up from the gibber, and the rest was bleached blond from the sun. The man had sun-narrowed eyes and ... Junia's heart sank ... a very stubborn chin. Time for another beauty check? But perhaps not. Perhaps he would be scornful of such things. He looked, from here, a very male man. No, she would just stand up and appear polite, alert, honest, and, if needs be, even deprecating.

She stood up.

The big table-top shuddered to a halt not far from her toes, and the driver and the man ... Mr Karl Kemble? ... got out.

'Good day,' said Junia pleasantly at once. 'Mr Kemble, I presume.'

'Well, it's not Livingstone,' the man answered in a slow, deep voice. He was looking Junia up and down as though, she thought resentfully, she was an unidentified object from outer space. 'Where in tarnation did you spring from?'

'Actually from the safari bus.'

'Were they sick of you? Did they detour from the Bitumen to drop you off here?'

'No, I came intentionally. You see, I'm on my way to Far-Off.'

'The devil you are! What do you want in Far-Off?'

11

Junia bit back a sharp rejoinder. If she was to get this hitch she was to do what Ned had said: smile. So she smiled.

'My fiancé is there, Mr Kemble,' she explained.

'Oh! Does he know?'

'Of course he knows. We're engaged.' She held up her left hand.

'I meant does he know you're coming?'

'Well, not exactly, but——'

'He doesn't know.' The man turned from Junia and began instructing the boy. The boy nodded and started depleting the pile of containers.

A minute went by. It came to Junia that more minutes were going to go by in just such unproductive silence unless she acted.

'I was wondering——' she broke in.

He took no notice.

'I was wondering——' she said louder.

'Yes, miss?'

'If you could take me.' There, it was out. She hadn't meant to say it so baldly, but something about this man cancelled sublety.

Certainly the answer he gave her was not subtle. He said shortly and definitely:

'No way.'

'I would pay, of course.'

'If I was taking you, you would do that ... of course ... but I'm not. Put that big chest more to the left, Jimmy, and all those smaller parcels can go into one large carton.'

'I can't stop here,' protested Junia.

'You should have thought of that before you left the bus.'

'I have to get to Far-Off,' she pleaded.

'To see a fiancé who doesn't know anything about

12

it? No, I'm sorry. My mistake. He *does* know about the engagement, you've just said so' ... a pause ... 'and showed me so, but he's not aware of the fact yet that you're following him up to make quite sure.'

She could have leaned forward and slapped his face, she felt so angry. Never, *never* had she been spoken to like this! She would tell Colin about him, warn him about him, as soon as she got to Far-Off. But to do that she had to get there first, and this—this pig was her only hope. Swallowing hard, she asked:

'Why won't you take me?'

'There's no call for me to answer any questions.'

'All the same I'd like to know. Is it me?'

'Yes.'

'But why?' she demanded. 'You don't even know me.'

'I know, or at least my eyes tell me' ... his eyes, bright blue once they emerged from their sun hollows, were estimating her boldly ... 'that you're female.'

'Well?'

'Females on these trips are disastrous. Hi, Jimmy, push that last load away from the tailboard.'

'Why?' persisted Junia. Well, she had to persist.

'They have to wash,' he said briefly.

'Presumably.'

'I mean they get hot and want to rinse their hands, and in no time they decide to shampoo their hair. There it hangs all wet and dripping, dripping over the load, over you yourself if you're near enough.'

'I don't think you'd ever be near enough.' She could not resist that.

'You're quite right, I wouldn't.' His voice was grim. 'Then they get headaches. Their make-up gets messy.'

'You sound as though you've had it all before,' she said dryly.

13

'I haven't, but I know how it goes.'

'Being a woman-hater?' Junia could see she would get nowhere, so she decided at least to give herself the satisfaction of talking back.

'I'm not answering that, I'm not obliged to, but I am giving you some advice.'

'I don't want it.'

'You're getting it all the same. Wait here with Ned for a southbound bus ... Ned will get on the pedal radio and ask for one to detour for you. But before that, realise this, miss, that Far-Off is no sentimental rendezvous for heartsick lovers. All it consists of is holes in the ground, sand, grit, gibber, heat and men.'

'You mean I'll be the only woman?' Junia inserted pertly.

'If I permitted you to go——' he began.

'Permitted?'

'If I permitted you to go you would have been the second woman. But it's stopping at one. Oh, yes' ... grimly ... 'it's certainly stopping at one. Finished that lot, Jimmy? Then nip into Ned's office and make us a cuppa. We'll grab it and then turn round at once. You' ... he looked at Junia ... 'can go across to Ned and break the news that he has now a star boarder. You can tell him, too, we're too busy today for a yarn.' He turned away, a tall, lean but very strong man, and made it to Ned's office in several loping strides.

For a few angry moments Junia stood looking after him. Would she try again? Would she go across to the office and put some dollar bills in front of him? Perhaps she could even corner Jimmy——

Then it came sharply to her that although the office was not far away, it faced the other way. That there were no windows for anyone to look out and see what she was doing.

14

She stood very still for a few watchful moments, then, satisfied, she transferred her attention to the large truck. Jimmy had loaded it well, placed back the protective canvas, but ... and Junia's heart leapt ... there was still a confined but sufficient space. Sufficient for one rather under-average-size girl.

Yes, she could do it. She *knew* she could do it, What was more, she was going to do it. There would be no room for her pack, but she wouldn't need it any more. Just a comb and lipstick. Surely Far-Off, for all that man's disparaging words, would be able to sell her a fresh shirt.

She picked up the pack noisily. It would give the impression that she was carrying it across to Ned's as that man had said. She did carry it a few steps, as far as the tank stand. Then she about-turned, sprinted back and hauled herself silently into the truck. She climbed under the canvas and waited. He had said they would turn round at once.

It was not long before they emerged again, but long enough, Junia rejoiced, for *that man* to believe she had taken his advice and gone across to Ned's. The man would glance across, she thought, she would be out of sight, and that would be enough.

'All aboard!' she heard him calling at that moment, and presently she felt movement, very uncomfortable movement even this early in the trip. It was not, she suspected, going to be fun and games.

But at least she was on the way, on the way to Colin. In Colin's arms later she would laugh over it all, not shudder at the horror strip that it was already beginning to prove. In Colin's arms all would be well.

Junia leant back, prayed that Jimmy's loading was secure and that none of the containers would fall on her, hoped for sleep.

She was still praying and hoping four hours later, only this time the prayers and hopes were being challenged by unbearable heat. It was the canvas, she supposed, added to the inland's worst period of the day. Four o'clock in the evening, the doomed rays of the sun doing their utmost, was always a torrid hour. Surely, *surely* Far-Off could not be much further. Even allowing for detours it must loom up fairly soon.

The sweat was pouring off her. At this rate, she thought, I'll soon be dehydrated. If only I could get a breath, put a finger out, feel I'm not entirely enclosed and cut off. She groped around and actually found a gap in the canvas. She put out her finger and felt a little better at once. She peered out, but that was unsuccessful, for all she got was sand in her eye. She did the finger stunt again, and then she forced off her sandal and poked out a big toe. It was beautiful. It was simply heavenly to feel fresh, if hot, air on you after the stuffiness of the canvas, even if it was only on your big toe.

Then something as well as air was touching her toe. Something was grasping it. Some animal? Some reptile? Junia had to bite back a scream.

A scream would have been disastrous just now, for the truck had stopped. Probably Jimmy was filling the radiator, or that man was checking the tyres, or——

She felt that pressure again on her big toe. She tried to withdraw the toe, but she found she couldn't. Whatever it was out there had a firm grip. Was she about to be stung? Bitten? Even chewed? Her scream was very close now.

But it never came. A gasp did instead. Still holding on to her toe, the toe-holder pulled back the canvas . . . and Karl Kemble stood looking down at her.

16

She saw him drawing a deep breath, a very deep breath, and she braced herself for his onslaught.

It was a long time coming. He must be summoning every abuse he could think of to throw at her. Then he spoke, and Junia knew that no abuse could be worse than what he did *not* say to her but what he *did* say to Jimmy.

'All right, Jimmy,' he called, 'turn the truck back. We're going back to Far-Flung. Yes, I said *Far-Flung*, man. At once!'

He wheeled now to Junia and he finished with ice:
'To put the lady *off*.'

CHAPTER TWO

'Back to Far-Flung!' Two voices said it in unison, said it in shock and dismay. Junia said it; Jimmy did.

Jimmy added to his protest: 'It will delay the load, Boss, and people are waiting for it.'

'You heard what I said, Jimmy.'

'Yes, Boss.'

'You, too.' The man had turned on Junia.

'Yes, Boss.' It was out before she realised it, and she put her hand to her mouth.

Jimmy still hesitated, and though he did not speak his dark liquid eyes pleaded with Karl Kemble. Junia was to learn later that some of the load was intended for his own camp, that his tribe, some kilometres out of Far-Off, eagerly awaited his return.

Junia pleaded herself, but not with her eyes, for they were uncontrollably stormy. Instead she reasoned aloud the foolishness of going back just to put her off.

'Then we'll leave you here,' Kemble shrugged. 'Back to the wheel, Jimmy.'

But Jimmy didn't, of course. His nature matched the softness of his eyes, and those eyes, and not Junia's argument, won the issue for the two of them.

'All right, we keep going,' Kemble said. 'I'll drive till we make camp, Jimmy. You take the lady's place between the containers. I have a few things to say to our passenger.'

His voice was grim, and Junia might have blanched

at what the grimness promised had she not been alerted by something else. 'Till we make camp,' he had just said. Surely he didn't mean they would not reach Far-Off tonight?

'How far is Far-Off?' she asked a little tremulously.

'As the crow flies, half an hour. But as we have to detour now, over gibber, over sand, over rivers, over logs, round trees, round outcrops, past mulga, through spinifex, over old dried bones now lying wet after the Wet, rimming brimming lagoons, I'd say——' He paused, deliberately she knew.

'You'd say?'

'Another twenty-four hours.'

'Another——'

'Yes,' he told her, and barely giving her time to jump in the passenger's seat, he released the brake.

At least the front seat was an improvement to the confined corner she had occupied for five bone-weary-ing hours. On the other hand you just didn't imagine horror stretch country, you saw it. You were in an entirely alien world. To make it more unreal, the recent rains had brought with them showers of flowers the desert had never known before and didn't know how to handle now. It was strange to look out on rough bluebush wreathed with white daisies, on skeleton fern hanging in pink lupin.

'It's beautiful.' She said it spontaneously, and became aware at once that he had taken his eyes off the rutted track a moment to look at her.

'Yes, but that's not what I asked you,' he said.

'Did you ask me something?'

'I asked you what the heck do you think you're at?'

He was detouring round a sandhill. How he found any track she would never know, she could only see sand. Sand with patterns on it, each pattern suggesting another route.

He must have read her thoughts. 'No,' he said, 'not roads, just wind whims.'

'I'm not "at" anything,' she told him, answering his question, 'I just have to go to Far-Off, that's all.'

'Lucky fellow.' Now he negotiated an outcrop of rock. 'Or is he, Miss—what was your name again?'

'It wasn't again,' she retorted childishly.

'Miss?'

'West.'

'Suitable,' he drawled. 'You're certainly west out here—north-west. Go west, young woman. But before West?'

She hesitated, not because of his impertinent question, though that ordinarily would have annoyed her and made her hesitate, but because Junia was such an unusual name and always invited a comment.

'June,' she mumbled.

'Are you sure?'

She looked at him in surprise; guilt as well as surprise. 'How can you know?'

'I don't know, but you don't look like a June to me.'

'How should June look?' she questioned.

'Long-stemmed roses and rhyming with moon. You're more outdoorsy.'

'Thank you,' she said coldly.

He shrugged, and a few bumps went by.

'So what is the real name?' he persisted presently.

'You wouldn't know it.'

'Try me.'

'It's Junia,' she admitted.

' "Salute Andronicus and Junia, my kinsmen, and my fellow-prisoners." *Romans*, 16, 7.' He dropped down a gear.

'You're a surprising man,' she commented.

'Why?'

'You know all that, yet you don't practise what you read.'

'I presume you are referring to the New Testament?'

'Yes.'

'Then give me an instance, please, Junia West.'

'You have no love of people,' she said nastily.

'Prove it.'

'You dislike women,' she went on.

'I do?'

'You sounded like it.'

'Then you must be right, of course. Now why do I dislike them? A simple question, really, suggesting a simple answer ... except, Miss West, there is none. None simple, I mean. No, it's more involved, more devious than that. I dislike them because they're sly, underhand, secretive, calculating, false, outwardly soft but inwardly as hard as nails.'

'I'm sure they're not.'

'Then don't be so sure. Also don't channel the conversation to me. We were discussing *you*, Miss West. How dared you stow yourself away like that?'

'I told you—I had to get to Far-Off.'

'Boy-friend dying?' he jeered.

'No.'

'Then dying to see you? No, that's not true, either. He doesn't even know you're coming.'

'There can be other reasons,' she shrugged.

'Give them to me.'

Junia was silent. How could she attempt to explain her woman's point of view to this very male man? She was not sure she could even explain it to herself. She *was* pursuing Colin, she supposed. You could put it in different words, but in the end it came to that. She was following him up.

But half a year, her thoughts ran on, had been a long time, too long a time. Oh, there had been letters, quite graphical letters, but never once had Colin said: 'Come.' Never once had he written down: 'I am coming to you.'

Her friends had married. Girls in the office had asked her curiously: 'When?' Suddenly she had known she had to know when herself—so—so she had left. It had been as simple and as basic as that.

To her surprise, after a quick searching look at her Karl Kemble did not probe that sensitive corner any more. He began talking about the country around them, and except that she knew that this tough outback man had nothing soft in him she would have said he was considering her. But Karl Kemble considerate! Junia felt hysterical laughter rising somewhere.

He was pointing to a formal gate front. There were comparatively few front gates up here, he said, since the homestead that a gate presumably should lead to would be too far distant from the track, so that an enclosing fence with slip-rails would suffice instead. One of these north-west properties, he added, could have eaten up the United Kingdom, and there were several more almost as large.

This gate bore a message. Unlike the Keep Outs and the Please Shuts Junia had seen from the coach, this one broke into rhyme.

> 'I was summonsed once for speeding,
> A procedure which I hate,
> But the charge will be for murder
> If you don't shut this flaming gate.'

'I suppose gates are important,' Junia agreed.

'More important here than anywhere else because you have cattle to get out and break a leg in some hole a prospector has left behind.'

'Yes,' said Junia abstractedly. She had learned all about the inland during the safari and now her mind was on something else. It was on tonight. When they made camp what would she do? She had left her pack under the tank stand at Far-Flung. She had only what she stood up in ... or bumped around in at this moment. That, and a comb and lipstick.

'How did you make out on the trip up?' Karl Kemble asked idily.

'Fine. It was my chore to gather the wood while my partner pitched the tent.'

'Partner?' He raised his brows steeply.

'*She* was good at pitching tents,' Junia said coldly.

'Pity you haven't got *her* tonight.'

'Yes,' said Junia, keeping as stiff a face as his. He must know by now that she had brought nothing with her.

Half an hour later they struck water. It was not the Lucy, Karl Kemble said, but a large clay pan that had filled up from the Wet.

'We can't cross it, so we have to go round it. It puts another eight hours on our schedule. Look, there's a phenomenon for you: Gulls. Seagulls this far inland! There are swans, too, tern, pelicans, no longer just harriers and hawks. It all happened after the long rains.'

It was very pretty, Junia thought. Bushes and rock outcrops punctuated the new inland lake, and every one of them was vine-festooned and studded with flowers.

'I reckon Nature must have been busting herself to show what she could do with the "dead" inside,' Karl

Kemble said. 'I think this site will do us again.' He pulled the large table-top to a halt.

'You're stopping?' Junia asked.

'Stopped.'

'On the coach we waited till two fingers from sunset.' Junia indicated with her own horizontally-placed fingers.

'You're not on the coach now, you're not playing explorers, you're doing the real thing. This is as good a camp as we'll find in hours. We've tried it before so we'll sample it again. Besides, our fence is up.'

'Fence?' she queried.

'There.' He nodded casually to a low enclosure.

'What's that for?' she asked.

'For us, of course, to keep out any crocs.'

'Any what?'

'Crocodiles.'

'But crocodiles aren't here,' she said.

'I'll admit they're generally further north, but if gulls can come down, they could, too. Anyway, we take no risk.'

'But a low fence like that!'

'A croc will not climb any fence,' he said definitely, and swinging himself out of the cabin he began to unpack what he and Jimmy would need for the night. Junia, with nothing to unpack, got out more slowly. She stood uncertainly for a few moments, then asked humbly if she could gather some tinder.

'Yes, go ahead. You'll want something to cook your steak by.'

She gulped. 'I haven't a steak.'

'Chops, then,' he tossed, and went round the truck kicking each wheel in turn, examining the pressure, then giving directions to Jimmy.

Because she couldn't just stand there, Junia began gathering sticks.

'Watch out for Joe Blakes,' Karl Kemble called. 'There's a few around since the Wet, and, like the flood flowers, a lot of them are alien crop. We all know our own fellers, the browns, the tigers, the diamonds, but the new blokes have got us licked.'

Even as he warned her, Junia stepped back from a windswept waste of leaves piled up under a stunted tree. She had intended to gather an armful of the dry tinder to start the fire, but the reptile coiled in the rubbish had stirred at the man's voice.

She stared at it fascinated. She wanted to retreat, but found she couldn't.

The next minute she was startled by a violent thud of rock thrown at the tree. It broke the spell. Both she and the snake found movement. Junia did not see where the snake went, but she went into a rough bush jacket because the jacket was now right behind her. The man in the jacket said: 'Take it easy, he's gone.' Karl Kemble added: 'He could have been venomous, he could have been harmless. I always like to give them the benefit of the doubt, and that's why I throw first. After all, they don't come looking for us.'

'I hope not!' Junia shuddered. 'I'd never sleep if I thought of that.'

'Why worry? You'll be zipped up in your sleeping bag.'

'Yes,' said Junia faintly, 'my sleeping bag.'

He gave her a narrow look but said nothing.

'Jimmy's got the fire going,' he said presently. 'Too early to throw your steak in yet ... no, chops, wasn't it? ... you'll have to wait for the embers. But you could brew a billy of tea.'

'I—I haven't any tea,' she faltered.

'Nor sugar. Nor a billy. Nor steak, chops, a sleeping bag, a tent. In short you have nothing, have you, Miss Go West Young Woman?'

'No,' Junia admitted.

'So you're scrounging on us?'

'Not at all, I can go without.'

'As far as I'm concerned you can, but look at Jimmy, like all his noble race he has a gentle heart. He'd choke over the first mouthful if he saw you had none. Anyway, we'll thrash it out over a cup of brew.' He walked back to where Jimmy was pouring hot water on to black leaves, and Junia followed him. Followed him very humbly.

The tea was wonderful. She cupped the mug in both hands and drank eagerly. She was not aware *how* eagerly until she felt Karl Kemble's eyes on her and looked back at him. He was grinning at her.

It was getting dark now. Last week on the safari they would all have been gathering round the fire by now, singing songs, telling stories, exchanging jokes. Junia wished desperately that she was back at last week, certainly not with this woman-hating man now taking over the role of cooking from Jimmy and doing wonderful, experienced things with steaks as big as plates. They must be experienced things, because the savour of the meat was tormenting Junia. I haven't eaten since this morning, she thought.

'Get this into you.' He handed over a tin dish. As well as the steak there were foiled potatoes, a hunk of damper and another mug of tea.

'I——'

'Eat, Miss West.'

'Am I depriving anyone?' she asked.

26

'We always carry extra for stowaways,' he assured her. 'Now stow that away. You, too, Jimmy.'

'Yes, Boss,' said Jimmy, and he dug his teeth into the steak.

By the time they had finished it was quite dark, but any idea that Junia might have had that there was to be a campfire chat was dispelled by the appearance of sleeping bags. In leisurely fashion Karl Kemble unrolled the two of them, unzipped them.

'It's been a long day,' he said, 'it's another long day tomorrow. I'm turning in.'

'Goodnight, Mr Kemble. Thank you for the steak—and the snake,' Junia proffered humbly.

'Wrong order. The snake happened first. Sorry your bed's a large fit, but we think it better that way.'

'My bed? But—but there are only two beds.'

'Jimmy wouldn't be seen dead in a bag,' he told her, 'he kips under the truck.'

'Then why do you carry two bags?'

'For the same reason that we carry extra steaks. Western hospitality. Surely, Miss West, you've heard of that, of western hospitality.'

'North-west, and I still think I might be depriving Jimmy.'

'Good grief, he could have this one of mine if he wanted to, and I would double up with you in yours. It's a big enough bag.' He spoke quite casually, but Junia knew that had she looked up and been able to see through the night that she would have found him grinning at her again. A hateful, baiting grin.

She slipped into the bag, and it certainly was an ample one. He was a strange man, she thought, looking up at the stars, a man given to sudden changes of mood. Ruthless one moment, quite kind the next. Certainly not an ordinary man. She wondered why Colin

27

had never mentioned such a man in his letters. He was not a man you could not notice.

'You didn't say where your fiancé worked,' Karl Kemble called from his own bag.

'Far-Off, of course.'

'Naturally, but what division?'

'Division?' she queried.

'Geo? Wolfram or mica man? Nickel expert?'

'Oh, no, none of those.'

'A base job man, then? Clerical staff, maintenance, amenities? Now who have I got on my payroll who looks as though he could belong to you?'

'Your payroll?' questioned Junia.

'Ninety-nine per cent of Far-Off depends on my pay packets,' he explained.

'I see.' Junia did not say more than that.

He waited a while, then when he spoke again she guessed he was leaning on an elbow and looking in her direction, for his voice was clearer ... and sharper.

'Not on my payroll, eh?'

'I didn't say so.'

'But you didn't say that he was on.'

Junia paused a moment. 'As a matter of fact, no, he's not. He belongs to that one per cent.'

... What *did* Colin do? Junia was thinking. Frankly she was not at all sure. When first he had gone 'bush' it had been to write a weekly column for one of the mining papers; he had told her he had an assignment. But she had never read any of his articles, though a mining magazine was scarcely the kind of reading matter a girl took out on the bus, or leafed over during lunch at the office.

'Name of?' Karl Kemble must still be leaning on his elbow, for his voice still came clear ... and sharp.

'Colin. Goodnight, Mr Kemble.' She tried to make her own voice sound halfway to sleep.

If she did do that, it still did not help her. He demanded: 'What comes after Colin?'

She gave away any thought of sleeping subterfuge and instead enjoyed the luxury of answering him back, for enjoyment was what it gave her.

'According to you,' she said triumphantly, 'I do.'

'After Colin, Miss West?' he persisted.

'Brent. He's Colin Brent. I shall be Mrs Colin Brent. Satisfied, Boss?'

He did not reply, but it wasn't because he slept, for although it was now pitch dark she knew his sun-narrowed blue eyes were burning across at her. She could almost feel their heat.

Well, I've stopped him, anyway, she gloated. He probably pictured Colin as some little pen-pusher far down in his wretched employ, snapping to attention whenever Big Boss said the word, whereas Colin is independent, just as physically big ... and far more good-looking ... as that outdoors man.

'Colin Brent.' The man spoke at last.

'Yes. Do you know him?'

'Everyone in Far-Off has to know everyone.'

'So you know Colin?'

'... I know him.'

There was a long silence that in the end Junia found she had to break.

'Well, it's Colin I'm going to,' she said.

No comment.

'Goodnight, Mr Kemble.'

No answer.

'Mr Kemble——'

She had an odd feeling that she was speaking to space, and at that moment the moon emerged from a bank of cloud and she saw that his bag indeed was empty.

Curiously uneasy, not triumphant any more, Junia turned on her side, and presently she slept.

CHAPTER THREE

JUNIA woke to a crystal-clear morning. As Sam, the coach-driver, had said, the inland had not yet heard of blue skies and soft air; in some instances the inland had not even heard of man and what he can do to beauty. *Her* men, however, Junia thought proudly, were doing nothing. They were leaving the campsite exactly as it would have been when first they had found it, and that was a pretty bank by a rippled lake. Only the small croc fence showed that someone had been here before.

Junia, sitting up in the big sleeping bag and accepting a large mug of tea, pointed out that they had not needed the croc deterrent.

'How would you know?' Karl Kemble said. 'You snored all night.'

'I'm sure I didn't!' she said indignantly.

'Well, you slept like a baby.'

'How would you know?' Junia used Karl Kemble's words. 'Didn't you sleep yourself?'

'Enough,' he evaded, and took away the mug and handed her another big tin dish of steak.

'I don't eat first meals.'

'You do now or go without. We serve no continental breakfasts here.'

'Yet it is a continent,' she pointed out.

'Stop arguing and eat your tucker.' He accompanied the advice with a grin, so Junia complied, and found she enjoyed it.

'As soon as you're ready we'll push off,' Karl Kemble told her.

'I'd like a wash,' she said hopefully.

'The lake awaits you, madam. It's quite pure, you won't come out in spots. Here's soap and a towel.' He handed them across.

Junia went down to the bank and knelt over the water. It was pleasant soft water and she would have liked to have stripped and immersed completely, but she made do with her arms, face and neck, paddling her feet as she soaped and dried. She wondered what she looked like. As with most girls, foundation, shadow and blusher had become as routine as cleaning one's teeth. As regarded those teeth, she rubbed around them as best she could with a corner of the towel, consoling herself that one or two brushing omissions should not comprise a disaster. She combed her hair, then she found a still spot in the water and used that water for a looking glass. What had he said yesterday? That she didn't look like a June, that June was long-stemmed roses and rhyming with moon. Instead she looked outdoorsy. Compliment or not? *Not*, she decided, regarding her reflection. She looked awful, she decided, quite barbarian.

But Karl Kemble, watching her come up to the camp again, caught his breath sharply.

'You look like the morning star, West.'

'I know. I saw myself.' Junia's voice was doleful.

'Have you seen a morning star?' he asked her.

'Yes. It's quite a raggedy number, isn't it? I mean, the evening star is pretty, and the night stars are diamonds, but the morning star ... well, it's just a fizzer.'

'Not here it isn't, it's——' But he didn't finish. He

had let down the tailboard and was climbing on and extending a helping hand to Junia to join him.

'I thought you might like to see things in reverse today,' he said, 'it's amazing what different aspects you get that way. Jimmy will drive.'

'Yes, that would be fun,' agreed Junia eagerly. 'Will it be bumpy, though? Should I hang on to something in case I fall off?'

'It will be bumpy, for which reason Jimmy will be going dead slow. If you can bring yourself to it you can hang on to me.'

'Thank you. It will be better than hurtling to the ground.'

He made no comment on that comment, and, as Jimmy proceeded along the unmarked track, it came to Junia that the man was much gentler today. Almost— why, almost solicitous.

He did not bother to tell her about the country they were passing through, he knew she would already have learned most of that on the safari. But he had lots of bits of pieces on stones and rock outcrops that Sam hadn't had, and Junia listened with interest.

'Look, there's a sign for you,' he said once.

'Sign?' she queried.

'Of nickel. Nickel fortunately gives out signs where most of the other stuff is pure hazard. Opals, for instance.'

'I can't see any signs.'

'That gossan.' He pointed.

'Gossan?'

'It's brown iron silica, and though it's not certain it can be a strong indication.'

'Are you a geologist?' asked Junia.

'No, but being with them rubs off. I started on the

administrative side of a company who sent me out to Far-Off, then promptly lost interest in their project, but by even that short a time the place had grabbed me, so I stopped on, and ... well, now it's mine.'

'You bought it?'

'It broke me, but it was worth it.'

'The return, you mean.'

'No, not that yet, but we're headed that way. No, I was really referring to the feeling,' he explained.

'The feeling you have for it?'

'Yes.'

'Yet you run it down, belittle it.'

'Do I?'

'You told me awful things about it,' she went on, 'you said holes in the ground, sand, grit, gibber, heat and men.'

'I also said it was no sentimental rendezvous for heartsick lovers,' Karl Kemble reminded her.

'Perhaps,' insinuated Junia shrewdly, 'you really just want to keep it to yourself.'

'Well, I will admit I would like to do all the picking,' he nodded.

'Picking?' she questioned.

'Of those who share Far-Off with me.'

'But surely you pick your own staff?'

'My own staff, yes, but——' His voice trailed off and he did not finish. Not that he needed to finish, Junia thought. He and his project represented ninety-nine per cent of Far-Off, he had told her, so he must be referring to the remaining one per cent—including Colin? *Only* Colin? She glanced sideways at him, found his jawline too uncompromising for a question, so started off on another tangent.

She found him easy to talk to, but she had the same odd impression as she had had earlier: that he was

34

being intentionally considerate and kind to her. Why was he being kind? she wondered. He was not what she would call an instinctively kind man.

He called to Jimmy to pull up while he showed her an ancient aboriginal waterhole, or wurlie. There were old pad-marks of dingoes leading to it—old, since following the Wet the animals had not needed to travel here to drink any more, there had been water everywhere.

But long before the animals, Karl Kemble told Junia, there had been the natives. That cleft of water had been their life source. They had all gone now, mostly to missions, so that the wurlie lay undisturbed in its rock basin, and instead of quenching human or animal thirsts, it trapped corners of sky and cloud by day, later handfuls of stars.

'Including my raggedy morning star?' Junia laughed.

'If we were out another night I'd waken you in the small hours, woman, and show you an "Inside" morning star.'

'I'll believe you,' Junia said a little breathlessly. For some reason she found herself looking away from him.

During the morning they actually did run into a tribe. So not all the First Australians, Junia observed, had gone to missions.

Karl Kemble looked at her in surprise. He and Jimmy handed out copious supplies to the tribe, so Junia knew now why one more in the truck had created no difficulty. Once more they were bumping along the track.

'First *Australians*?' Karl Kemble picked her up.

'That's what I said.'

'But you're wrong. They are very possibly, very probably, even the first men.'

She looked at him in incredulity, and he nodded.

'Anthropologists believe so, they believe the Java man, who has been established authentically as the beginning of it all, walked here ... he could have done that in the Ice Age ... and so it all started. It's a very wonderful thing. It's also a sobering thought.' Instinctively he had taken her hand in his in his enthusiasm, and just as instinctively Junia left it there, feeling the solemnity and marvel, too.

'Imagine this,' he went on. 'There had been a culture here for years and years before the Pyramids were built. These first men of all had had their own enlightenment for a very long time.'

Junia listened eagerly. She liked him like this. Not sarcastic, taunting, as when they first had met, on the other hand not deliberately kind as somehow she felt he had set himself out to be, instead lit up with something as thrilling and elemental as life itself.

It did not last, of course. A subject so profound could not last. He asked her offhandedly why she hadn't told her fiancé she was coming.

'I wanted to surprise him,' she explained.

'He's been there six months' ... so he knew that much of Colin ... 'why didn't you surprise him before?'

'Colin thought it might be rough for me at Far-Off.' —Colin had said that once, Junia recalled—'he said he'd be down'—he had said that, too. She asked quickly, too quickly, if there had been many women at Far-Off.

'Never many,' Karl Kemble drawled. 'A few wives who didn't last, a cook who we saw also didn't last after what she showed us she could do with good food. Then' ... a pause ... 'my fiancée.'

'Your——' Junia stopped herself. Of course he would

have a fiancée, he was attractive enough in his aggressively masculine way to have a harem of fiancées.

'That sole woman now?' she inquired politely.

'Yes.'

'She is your fiancée.'

'I said so.' Another pause. 'She is also my secretary. Or should I say I have a secretary who is my fiancée? It's another example of which comes first, isn't it? The secretary? The fiancée?' He laughed, but somewhere there was a note that was not laughter.

Because they had made better time than they had estimated, lunch was a leisurely affair with the prospect of a rest afterwards.

'Jimmy will be pleased,' grinned Karl Kemble, 'he's generally as alert as a spy plane, but he still relishes an after-meal nap.'

'I feel relaxed myself,' admitted Junia. 'But what do you mean by spy plane?'

'I mean spy plane. Usually it's a small craft, possibly a Cherokee or Cessna. It goes over a digging and puts two and two together.'

'I don't understand you,' she said.

'If the gang is working, then something is doing, if the gang has left, then there's nothing worth reporting.'

'Reporting to whom?'

'The ones who charter the spy plane and pay for the information.'

'But that's awful!' Junia exclaimed.

'Awful, yes, yet not so awful. At least we see the spying being done. It's what we don't see being done that does the harm.' Karl Kemble's voice had changed, and glancing at him Junia saw his brooding look.

Jimmy had stretched out under the trunk and was already asleep.

'The men work hard,' Karl Kemble told Junia, 'it's

blood and sweat all the way when you choose the job of digging holes. They don't mind the hummers and hangers-on so much. One has to expect that element in a project ... just as one has to expect a certain degree of spying, and at least, the men say, the spies are doing their dirty work in the open. Every time a spy plane goes over they give it their clenched fist, but they still don't hate them all that much. But they do hate the cheats, and every project always seems to have a cheat—someone sly, and in the know, someone whom you can't put your finger on. News somehow leaks out, finds leak out. But no one can ever discover the leak.'

'Has Far-Off its leak?' Junia asked carefully.

'Yes,' he answered just as carefully.

'Can't you stop it?'

'No.' He came in abruptly and at once. 'At least—not yet.'

There was a silence. During it Jimmy emitted a loud snore.

'Thank heaven,' Junia said more to herself, 'that my Colin is in that one per cent.'

'What do you mean by that?' asked Karl Kemble.

'He doesn't belong to your outfit, Mr Kemble,' Junia pointed out.

'No, he doesn't belong.'

'In which case,' Junia continued, 'Colin couldn't ... it wouldn't be possible——'

'Yes?'

'What you just said.'

'Finish it,' he ordered.

'He couldn't cheat. He couldn't know what was going on.'

'No,' said Karl Kemble, 'that's how it looks.'

It wasn't a full answer. Junia waited for more, but nothing came. She lay back, closed her eyes as Karl

Kemble now had done, pretended sleep, but it was only pretence, she felt oddly disturbed.

They set off again in the early afternoon. Karl Kemble said they should make Far-Off in a few hours.

The country was pleasantly hilly now. Karl told Junia that occasionally the west did things like this; he said there could be miles of dead flat, then suddenly welcome undulations would take over before a descent to a sanded, or gibber, level once more.

This elevation consisted of knolls and hummocks with small hollows between them, and the afternoon sun, striking between the gully walls, brought out the aromatic smell of the desert underbrush.

'It's lovely, it's herby,' appreciated Junia, taking deep breaths.

'It's Australian bush, and one day I'm going to break away from projects to bottle toilet products, after-shaves, all that, and I shall call my baby just that. Australian Bush.' He was grinning, but she could see he had given it some thought.

'Australian Bush,' she experimented. 'Yes, I like it.'

They left the elevation and began pushing through the red dust and skeleton weed again. How Jimmy found one track in the millions of dune tracks, Junia would never know ... nor did Jimmy know a few minutes later when he misjudged one of the wind patterns as their accustomed detour but went down instead into a sharp rut and promptly found himself bogged.

Bogged among the dust and the skeleton weed sounded unbelievable until you remembered the long recent Wet. Junia stood by while Karl Kemble laid down a rough mat he said he always carried for moments like these while Jimmy roared the engine and tried to force the truck out. But with each attack the truck only went deeper in. They lightened the load to no avail. Kemble and Junia shoved without result. They dug round the bog, but still nothing happened.

They had lingered longer than necessary over lunch since they had believed they had only a few hours to go. Now, with the usual rapidity of the near-tropics, night came on them before they realised that day was over.

'That's it, Jimmy,' called Karl at last, 'we'll have to make it a day. And' ... with an oblique glance at Junia ... 'another night.'

'Yes, Boss,' Jimmy said.

'I didn't hear *you*, Miss West,' Karl reminded her.

'Yes, Boss,' Junia complied quite readily. She was puzzled with herself, she wanted to get this journey over, she wanted to get to Colin, and yet the delay came with an almost heady excitement to her, no dismay at all. Why ... oh, *why*, she thought, was she feeling like this?

The same as last night, Jimmy built a fire, and once more steaks were produced.

'We carry a refrigerator, paraffin variety, in case you're puzzled over the seemingly never-ending supply of goodies,' Karl explained. 'Often we have perishable stuff aboard to take back to Far-Off. The freezer is the reason why we're never stuck for an extra helping along the track. Sorry we have no lagoon as we did last night to provide you with your morning wash, though, but we can promise you a tinful of water.'

'Thank you. Can't I do anything to help?'

'You can set out the sleeping bags. Jimmy will sleep like he always does, under the truck. We'll sleep against that rock, I think.'

'Crocs?' she queried.

'No water around, unless you count Jimmy's bog.'

'How will you get out of that?'

'The mud will dry up a little overnight, yet not enough to imprison us, but I hope enough to let us prise ourselves forward instead of squelching downwards as we were doing just now. Anyway, mornings always bring new hope, don't you think?'

'I don't know,' admitted Junia. 'I doubt if I've ever thought about it.'

'No, lovers only think of nights,' he agreed, and proceeded to throw on the steaks.

When the meal was over, Karl did not suggest turning in at once as he had the previous evening. Instead he and Junia sat staring into the campfire, gazing at the plush darkness behind the fire that now waited, like a stage awaits its principal actor, for the moon to appear.

'This country needs its melon moons and blobs of stars,' Karl said musingly, 'for it goes mostly for earth colours and nothing oatmeals, that is once away from the red rocks, so there has to be some levity.'

'Just now it doesn't go for drabness,' said Junia. 'Now it's a wilderness of blossom.'

'That's not its usual behaviour. But then we, mankind, are not treating it usually either. We're digging it up, probing it, delving into it. No wonder it's resisting by doing everything it's never done before. 'Tell me' . . . with an abrupt change of topic . . . 'where you planned to stop in Far-Off.'

'I—I hadn't planned. But there would be a hotel?'

'No.'

'Oh,' Junia said.

'No hotel, no motel, no lodging house—but a hostel.'

'Then——?'

'For the workers,' he said.

'But Colin is at Far-Off,' she pointed out.

'And has rented an empty project unit, one of the

pre-fabs that a discontented wife occupied before she got fed up and pushed off.'

'Then——?'

'But there are no more available,' Karl Kemble said definitely. 'We're using them as offices.'

Junia was silent for a few moments. Presently she said: 'I think Colin may be able to find me something with him.'

'Scarcely conventional.'

'Conventions in such a remote place?' she commented.

'You could be surprised,' Karl suggested.

'In which case I'll marry Colin at once.'

'You'd have to wait for our dog-collar man, and we've had the Reverend Bill Flett only last month. Another six weeks before he returns. Can convention stand that?'

'I'll camp, then. Or doss under a tree.'

'Determined, aren't you?'

'No—I mean yes. I mean——'

'I don't think you know what you mean,' grinned Karl Kemble. 'But not to worry. We'll find you a bed at the hostel. Like the steaks we carry, we can always produce a bed. Well, I suppose we'd better get some rest.'

They both slipped into their bags, but Junia found herself lying wide-eyed staring at the sky. Karl's words had dismayed her. She had expected a hotel of some sort. She had taken it for granted. But come to think of it, Colin never had mentioned it. Yet ... thoughtfully ... what *had* Colin actually mentioned? Oh, there had been thrilling accounts of safaris, encounters with dingoes, kangaroos, wild buffalo, all the magazine things one reads, only much more enthralling when one knew the chief actor, but nothing ... well, nothing necessary and essential. Like—accommodation. Like—shops. Like—life itself.

'Don't the men drink?' she asked across to the other sleeping bag.

'Come along to our wet canteen one night,' he laughed back, then she heard him turn over as though the subject was closed.

She still lay wide-eyed and wide awake, though. For the first time she was wondering what she had put herself in for ... she was wondering how Colin would react to all this. Before she had been quite certain. No doubts at all. But now ...

She must have dozed at times for all her wakefulness, for when she became aware of the lights in the sky some time later it was a while before she could focus her eyes. But when she did so at last, she gasped.

'Karl——!' she called, not realising she had used his name. 'Karl, what's that?'

He sat up at once, and the next moment he was getting out of his bag and crossing to her.

'Don't be alarmed,' he said, 'you're seeing the Min-Min Lights, not a satellite, not a vision, not a reflection taken up by the night sky from a hundred miles away and flashed here. Nothing at all like that.'

'Then what?'

'Just something that happens, and few are lucky enough to see it. There's no explanation. Neither geos nor scientists nor even space men can say why. It simply occurs.'

'It's—it's mesmeric. I want to walk to it.'

She got up, but of course she did not walk to any lights. Instead, as though she had scrambled out of her bag for that purpose, she walked to Karl's arms, and after holding her very still for a long moment, he bent down and kissed her. As instinctively as she had got up to walk to the lights, Junia kissed him back. A long still moment went by before each stepped back.

Karl led her to the sleeping bag again. He tucked, then zipped her in. Never once as he did so did he speak. She did not speak to him.

It never happened. It never happened. That was the last thought that Junia thought before she slept.

In the morning the two men got to work on the bogged truck while Junia cooked the breakfast. Just as she slapped the steaks on the three dishes, the big truck came out of its bog.

'This time we'll really make Far-Off,' said Karl, coming back in triumph to take up his laden plate. 'Home to your Ludy tonight, eh, Jimmy? ... Miss West and her young man reunited?'

'Yes,' said Junia. She leaned over and added another steak to Jimmy's portion. She did not look at Karl. But she did remember to remind him of the morning star he had forgotten to show her.

'I didn't forget,' he denied. 'I thought you had enough on your plate.'

'Too much.' She had put her breakfast down on the ground.

'Not that plate,' he said.

When it came to moving off again, Karl put Junia beside him once more on the tailboard.

'You may as well get to know your future environs,' he said. 'Also after last night's bad show Jimmy will be taking it extra carefully, getting back into my good graces.'

'I don't believe he was ever in your bad ones,' smiled Junia.

'No, not Jimmy.'

They meandered over dry ridges and wet hollows,

44

over flats returning after long rains to red sand or gibber again. Karl drew Junia's attention to the erosion he said had been absent before. 'The Wet did it,' he accused.

'But wouldn't moisture, even too much moisture, benefit, not damage?'

'The damage comes in the quick drying. This part of the country just didn't know how to handle wet. But why should it, it had never had it before. You have to handle things, Junia West.' He had turned his attention from the landscape to the girl beside him. 'Do you think you'll be able to handle *your* situation?'

'Have I a situation?' she asked.

'Seeing your feller for the first time after six months I'd say yes, you do.'

'But I've had letters. Colin is a wonderful correspondent. He's a very gifted writer. That's how he got his columns for the mining magazines.'

'Oh, yes?' Karl encouraged.

'Have you read them?' Junia asked.

'Have you?'

'Well—no. I mean, women don't usually go for that sort of reading. But Colin's letters have been wonderful, graphic. His description of the country! All the exciting things he did!'

'Like?'

'Like?—Well, he met this unknown tribe once ... they made a veritable king of him. Then he was in a brumby incident, and a camel adventure. It all read like a book.'

'Probably was taken from a book.'

'What?' Junia turned furiously on him, and at once he apologised.

'Sorry. Take no notice of me.' A pause. An intentional one? 'But also, Junia West, don't take everything for granted.'

'What do you mean?' she demanded.

'I don't know what I mean,' he admitted, 'otherwise I'd be more explicit. But keep a cool head, girl. Remember you've been away from this feller——'

'His name is Colin.'

'Away for half a year. It can make a difference.'

'Not to us.' Now it was Junia who paused—why, she could not have said. She felt confident enough, but still she paused. Coldly, she asked: 'Is that all?'

'No.' The man spoke quite intently. 'Should you need me, simply come to me. Ask for Karl Kemble.'

'I know your name.' This time Junia's voice was icy. If she should need him indeed!

'Then *ask*,' he told her, and at the same time he jumped off the tailboard of the truck that was now proceeding almost at a snail's pace, and ran round to the front. Soon after he had climbed up beside Jimmy, the truck began to make a better pace, so he must have taken over the driving. Junia withdrew to a safer distance from the tailboard among the cartons and parcels.

She drowsed a little in the warm sun, and that was why she was unaware when the truck pulled up later in the afternoon to let Karl Kemble off. She only wakened, later again, when the engine gave a last shuddering, definite halt.

Jimmy had climbed down from the cabin and had come round to her.

'We're here, miss.'

'At Far-Off?'

'Yes.'

'It seems latish,' she said. 'Didn't you stop for lunch?'

'Boss wanted to make better time, so we pushed on.

46

We had a bite to eat on the move, but since you were asleep we left you like that.'

'Yes. Thanks.' Junia was looking around her, looking at rows of pre-fab buildings, looking at a very large, sprawling, one-storeyed pre-fab erection which she supposed would comprise the project hostel. She was looking at several pre-fab houses, done in the accepted pre-fab project style of four rooms deep and two rooms wide—Which one was Colin's?

'Where is Mr Kemble?' she asked Jimmy. 'I want to thank him.'

'He hopped off further back, miss. He said to show you Mr Brent's place. It's that last one down the row.'

'Then thank you, Jimmy,' Junia smiled. 'No doubt I'll see you later.' She accepted the bag Jimmy had taken down from the truck, grinned at him again, then began walking to Colin's pre-fab.

Thank goodness, she thought, it was that time of evening when nobody was about. Probably they were all at the canteen bar now, so there would be no curious eyes following her. She did not mind curiosity, in fact in a woman-starved situation like this it would have been uncomplimentary to her if they had not been interested, but first of all she wanted to find Colin.

When she reached the last house, the place was in darkness, and Junia's heart sank. Now she would have to go to the hostel after Colin, the hostel canteen, for there was nowhere else here that Colin could go.

She took up her bag that she had put down and was just about to retrace her steps when she heard movement somewhere. No, movements. More than one person. Two. No, she was wrong again. One.

It was Colin. Colin emerging at this moment and crossing to her. He was coming out of the shadows of

47

the verandah. He must have seen her in the last faint light of dusk.

'Good heavens, Junia,' he was saying, 'I just can't believe it!'

He was pulling her into the house ... pulling her a little roughly ... even urgently.

'I want to see you properly, my darling,' he was apologising rather thickly. 'It's been so long, so damn long. Oh, my Junia!'

He was kissing her, kissing her masterfully, not releasing her for a moment, and suddenly it came to Junia where this would have thrilled her a year ago, now it left her a little surprised. For Colin had never been like that, he had been a distinctly withdrawn man.

He had snapped on the light now to look at her, and again she was surprised, surprised at a room much more lavish than she had thought. It would have been lavish in Sydney, so out here—Well, good luck to Colin, he must have worked very hard for this.

She looked at Colin himself now. Not changed. Not changed at all. The same light hazel eyes, a little reddened from the hard climate, she supposed, his skin not as bronzed as she had imagined from his letters telling her of his exploits, even palish. Also ... yes, it was a fact ... a little rotund. A trifle ashamed of herself and her criticism, she leaned up and kissed him on her own account.

It was then she became aware of it. A subtle drift of jasmine. At least she judged it was jasmine.

'Col—' she began in amusement, for she was about to tell him that his taste in male colognes had certainly changed.

But he had her in his arms again, so tight she could not move, so close that she could not see. He rubbed his

48

head in her hair, an old endearment of his, he kissed her ears. He drowned out all sound with those kisses.

... So Junia did not hear the echo of quietly retreating steps outside the house.

CHAPTER FOUR

JUNIA was a little breathless by the time she emerged
at last from Colin's tight embrace. It was certainly an
emotional welcome, she thought ... but at the same
time she put aside another, and quite dismaying,
thought. There had been no magic for all the emotion
in it for her. She had waited for the old alchemy to
come. It had not.

'Why didn't you tell me, Junia?' Colin was asking,
apparently unconscious of any lack of response. 'You
shouldn't have sprung things on me like this.'

'In love it's always spring,' she reminded him fondly.
—Fondly? Such a pale word.

'Of course, but I would have preferred to have
known.'

'You mean you didn't want me here?'

'Hell, no, of course I wanted you, darling, but I—
well, I would have had things fixed up for you. As it
is——'

'As it is it all looks very wonderful to me, if you are
meaning your house, Colin. I didn't imagine you lived
in such comfort.' Again Junia was looking around her.

'It's a damn hard life, Junia,' said Colin defensively,
'a man deserves comfort.'

'Of course, Colin. And then, too, you had me in
mind, though I would still have come if it had been a
shack with an earth floor. Darling, if you've been working your fingers to the fabled bones just to pamper me,

that shack would have done equally well. No—better, Colin, if you'd only sent for me before.'

'I wanted perfection for you, my Junia, and now ... well, now you've really got me on the wrong foot.'

'What do you mean, Colin?'

'I wanted you to come *here*. Right here in this house. You can't now, of course.'

'Why not?'

'Why not?' He gave her a surprised look. 'Well, I hardly expected to hear *you* ask that.' He smiled whimsically at her, or rather he seemed to try for whimsy.

'And I hardly expected you to express such a conventional view, Colin, especially out in the Never-Never.' As she said it, Junia was thinking of someone else who had spoken practically the same words as Colin. Karl had, but not with whimsy ... contrived whimsy.

'These places are not what you think they are, Junia,' Colin was saying. 'My idea was to finish everything off, then go south and marry you.'

'Then I've saved you the trouble, Colin.'

'Of going down, yes, but—marrying?'

'Yes, Colin?'

'It's not as easy as down there with all those little churches round the corner.'

'Oh, I know about that, I know the minister only calls every few months, but there must be somewhere else, someone else. A district office. Some justice of the peace.'—Karl Kemble, Junia thought, would be certain to be one, even though he had not said so.

She became aware that Colin was looking at her rather narrowly, and she flushed. She thought of what Karl Kemble had said when she had protested that to be with Colin she would even camp out, sleep under a tree. He had drawled:

'Determined, aren't you?'

She had not known what to answer him, and now she did not know again should Colin speak to her in a similar strain. She actually found herself searching for explanatory words, only to fail to find them. She heard herself babble a little self-consciously:

'That scent, Colin. That drift of jasmine. It's you, isn't it? I never thought you would change your old cologne. A minty one, wasn't it?'

'I haven't changed. It's not me, it's the smell of the underbrush, of course.'

'Underbrush?' she queried.

'The bush.'

'Yet it's very sweet.'

'Yes.' Colin was lighting a cigarette, quite composed again now, smiling at Junia through the weave of smoke.

'Not tangy? Not herby?' she persisted.

'Darling, why all this idle chatter? Come here, you reckless sweet thing, for you must be reckless running after me like that. Oh, yes, Junia, you've run. By heaven, though, you're lovely. I hadn't remembered just how lovely.' For a moment there was an odd note in his voice that Junia could not place.

He drew her down on the couch beside him and looked admiringly at her.

'What to do about you, Junia?' he mused. 'I know what I want to do, but I am after all in a rather ticklish spot here.'

'You mean here at Far-Off?'

'Yes.'

'But how?'

'Well, I would be the sole one, I would say, not under Big Brother's watchful eye, which makes me all the more watched, if you follow me.'

'I don't. And who is Big Brother?'

'Name of Kemble—Karl Kemble. He practically owns the place. In fact you could call him Mr Far-Off.'

'Do you call him that?'

'I call him a lot of things,' Colin said blandly, 'none of them for your pink ears.' He kissed the ears. 'Are you tired, darling?' he asked at once. 'Those small planes buck like a bronco. Incidentally, how did you snare a flight? I know you have a pretty face, a persuasive look, but——'

'I didn't fly,' she told him.

'Didn't fly? but there's only one other way to come, and overlanding is taking two days now because of the detour.'

'Three,' Junia corrected.

'Three . . . you mean you actually did it?'

'Yes.'

'But how——'

'I came by truck from Far-Flung,' she explained.

'But that would have to be Big Brother's truck, there's no other transport, and *he* would never bring you. He takes a relief, but, like all the things up here, he does most of the operation himself, and K.K. is a stickler, and certainly would never permit a hitch.'

'Yet I'm here, aren't I?'

'You certainly are, darling. How?'

'I—well, I brought myself.'

'You what?'

'He . . . Mr Kemble . . . refused me, so I stowed away.'

'You stowed away on the truck?'

'Yes.'

'Did he stand for that? Don't tell me he didn't find you? Not in a two-day journey.'

'Three. Two nights. Oh, yes, he found me, but I was allowed to stay.'

'Keep on, pet, this is getting very interesting. Very, very interesting, as a matter of fact.' Colin sat closer to Junia. He put his arm around her.

'We were on the track three days and two nights,' Junia reported. 'We had a delay.'

'I bet you did!' Now Colin grinned suggestively.

There was something sick about the narrow smile and Junia felt herself withdrawing. A little sharply she said:

'Jimmy was there, too.'

'Of course, darling. Big Brother always takes some-one in case there's dirty work.'

'There was dirty work, and he worked as hard, and harder, than Jimmy. He——'

'Look, Junia, I don't want to discuss him. I don't like the man and he doesn't like me. It's a pity you ever came up here if it meant travelling with him, and yet . . . By George, yes!' Colin's eyes now had drawn a veil.

'What are you talking about, Colin?' Junia asked in confusion. She also asked it in inquiry, for Colin was disengaging himself from her, he was getting inten-tionally to his feet.

'Darling, I'll have to take you up to the hostel,' he said. 'They won't see you stuck.'

'I'm not stuck. I'm here with you.'

'But you can't stay here, Junia, and particularly now that——'

'Yes, Colin?'

'Particularly now that Big Brother knows you've come.' Colin said it smoothly and at once, but Junia had a shrewd idea it was not what he had started out to say.

Colin's arm was extended, he was preparing to con-duct her out. Stubbornly Junia sat on.

'I can't understand you,' she said.

'What is it you can't understand?'

'You made a cheap remark just now when you learned how I came.'

'Did I, pet? In what manner?'

'Well, it sounded like that to me, sounded cheap. And yet' ... before Colin could argue ... 'now you want me to continue the same way.'

'What same way, dearest?'

'Well—nearer to him than to you, which I must be up there. Nearer, I mean, to Karl Kemble.'

Colin had Junia on her feet now and he was ruffling her hair. 'I don't know if I care about that word "continue",' he reproved roguishly.

'You're misinterpreting me, Colin. If it was all right for—Big Brother, as you put it, for Mr Far-Off, wouldn't it be all right for you, my own fiancé, the man I'm going to marry—I mean, for me to stop here? I don't want to go to the hostel.'

'Nonetheless you are going, this is too good to miss.'

'What, Colin?'

'I really mean, sweet, that already being the watched one here I'm anxious to give no cause for any extra scrutiny.'

'But——'

'Come on,' Colin put his hand under Junia's elbow and guided her to the door. Again, if elusively, she was aware of that subtle drift of jasmine. It continued until they stepped outside into the night.

At once that herby, aromatic tang that Junia had experienced in the bush pushed the jasmine away. She raised her face to Colin to say so, to argue the difference, but at that moment a beam from some star caught his features, and she saw that he was pensive ... barely aware of her. Barely aware of a fiancée who had travel-

55

led nearly a thousand miles to be with him! Junia could scarcely contain a rueful laugh.

She did contain it, though. She looked up the road, if the rough track could be called that, and said dubiously: 'Are you sure I'll be accepted, Colin?' She knew she would be through Karl Kemble, boss, but would she be accepted through Colin Brent, camp outsider?

'Sure.' Colin had lost his preoccupation and was back with her again.

'Will the men be agreeable? I know it's a male régime except for——'

'Yes? Yes, Junia?' Colin said a little sharply.

'Except for Mr Kemble's secretary.'

'Quite true.'

'Who is also his fiancée.'

This time Colin did not concur with Junia. He said abruptly: 'He told you that?'

'Yes.'

A few moments went past in silence, any awkwardness being covered by Colin's helping of Junia over some rough patches. When Colin spoke again he was his usual confident self.

'Cheer up, my dear, you need have no qualms.'

'Qualms?' she echoed.

'About being in a male world. Renata will be there, too.'

'Renata is——?'

'She is the secretary.'

'Fiancée-secretary, or is it secretary-fiancée?' Karl Kemble had said something like that.

'Really, Junia, does it matter?' Colin's voice was irritated. 'I'm just trying to point out to you that you won't be establishing something new. A woman among men, I mean.'

'But will this Renata care for that? Girls always like to be the only one.'

'I think,' Colin said, 'when I explain to Rennie ... to Renata, that she will agree.'

'Agree?' It seemed to Junia that it was more the boss's prerogative to agree, or perhaps the hostel manager's job.

'Well, I don't know for sure, do I?' Again Colin sounded irritated. 'Renata could even have to share her room with you.'

'She wouldn't like that. I wouldn't like it myself. Isn't there any other way?'

'There may be. Just leave it to me, Junia. After I've had a talk with Rennie ... Renata ... I believe we can get somewhere.'

'Am I to gather,' observed Junia drily, 'that the Far-Off taboo on you doesn't stem from the secretary-fiancée, then?' Rennie ... Renata, she was thinking.

'There's no taboo, as you put it, even Kemble himself is civil, it's just—well——'

'But Renata is more than civil?' suggested Junia, wondering at herself as she suggested it, for it meant nothing at all to her, not worthy, anyway, of any innuendo.

'Renata is a very fine person. She has one of those friendly natures that must include everyone in spite of other attitudes. Here we are at the hostel now. We'll go to Renata first.'

'Not to Mr Kemble? Not to the hostel manager?'

'Both the same person—both Kemble. No, leave this to me,' Colin said again. He told Junia to wait, then he walked down a long passage, and later turned a corner into another passage.

There was nothing to see. There was no light to the street outside, very little light in the entrance hall, any

57

illumination, Junia supposed, was reserved strictly for where it was needed. No doubt conservation would be necessary in a self-supplying place like this. They would have it in bedrooms, in corridors, in ablution sections, in the common-room, from which there was now echoing the usual amount of noise that must occur when men gather together.

Someone was walking down the hall opposite to the one that Colin had taken. Junia shrank back. She was a friendly person, and liked meeting people, particularly, she had to admit, men, but she did not care for her present position. It made her appear almost—well, skulking, she fretted.

'Why, it's Go West, Young Woman.' The man belonging to the long leisured steps had stopped beside Junia. 'Come to take me up about that room?' Karl Kemble smiled.

'No. I mean, I do want it if I can still have it, but Colin is asking Renata.'

'Oh, is he now? And since when has Renata taken over the apportioning of accommodation?'

'I don't know,' said Junia a little uneasily, 'but Colin thought it possible that I might have to share a room with Renata, so of course he had to speak with her first.'

'Of course,' said Karl Kemble, 'it's only right that he speaks to her first.' He himself spoke so correctly that Junia looked up quickly. She saw nothing, though, just the same bland face.

'So,' observed the man presently, 'Brent wouldn't have you?'

'Nothing of the sort. He—he was just thinking of me, as you yourself, if you remember, also thought. He—he insisted on my being under a different roof.'

'But I didn't insist on that. Our roof out there was

the same, wasn't it, navy blue and set with stars.'

In the corridor's dim light Junia could see the stars. Big blobs of stars. He had said that. He had said a melon moon.

'But no unexplained lights.' He was following her glance. She had not known he was so near her. His voice came so clear she even gave a little start.

'Bad nerves,' he commented. 'The west will soon fix them.'

'I have good nerves,' she said. 'I've never been a tense person.'

'No, and you weren't out there in the bush.' He was silent for a brief moment. 'No, you were the morning star. I still haven't shown that to you, have I? How about tomorrow, Miss West?'

'I don't know if I'll be here.'

'You will be,' he assured her.

'I may disturb your secretary—I mean, your fiancée if we're in the same room.'

'You won't be,' he told her.

'It appears to me,' said Junia a little wildly, 'that it was a waste of time Colin asking your fiancée.'

'Her name is French.'

'Colin asking Miss French—it's you who supplies all the answers.'

'Of course I supply the answers. I own the place.'

'Ninety-nine per cent,' Junia reminded him deliberately. 'Oh, yes,' she continued, 'Colin has told me about you being Mr Far-Off.'

'Wishing as he said it that I *was* far off.'

'He didn't say so.'

'But then you haven't been with him long enough to find out, have you? Isn't that rather odd, Miss West? To dispose of a fiancée quite so quickly.'

'I haven't been disposed of. Also I don't know how

59

other fiancées are dealt with.—How do you deal with yours?"

She listened rather triumphantly for his answer. He was a very alert person ... sharp was her own adjective ... and it was challenging to get in a matching rejoinder. When he did not reply she turned round ... and he was not there. She could not have credited that such a large man could have moved away so quietly and so quickly. But Karl Kemble had. She was on her own again. No, not on her own. Two people were coming down the hostel corridor up which Colin had gone to speak with Renata French. Was this the reason Karl had left now? No, a man would not leave because of his fiancée.—But would Karl Kemble leave because of Colin?

But Junia had no time to pursue that thought. The pair were coming closer, and even in the restricted light Junia could see that Renata French was a very attractive and distinctive woman. Indeed, she would be one of the most beautiful girls she had ever met—tall, slim, regal, dark-haired, dark-eyed. Her voice, too, when she spoke, was winning. The low, warm timbre as she greeted Junia held no trace of resentment. There was nothing half-hearted in the firm grip of her hand.

'I'm glad you're here. You're just what I needed. Isn't that so, Colin?'

'Just what we *both* needed,' Colin assured her, and Junia's heart went out to them for their welcome. Perhaps that man, that Kemble, *was* Mr Far-Off, *did* have the last word, perhaps she would have been given accommodation without Renata's help, but it took nothing away from her sensation of being wanted, something *he*, Karl Kemble, certainly had been at pains not to show.

'Thank you,' Junia appreciated. 'Thank you very much. Can I call you Renata?'

'Of course, Junia. Now I'll show you your room. It's next to mine. Is that all right?'

'It's wonderful. I didn't want you to be asked to share.'

'My dear, that would have been no infliction. Come now, and I'll give you the legend. Isn't that what they say at the bottom of maps, Colin? The legend? No, Colin, you can't come.' He had started to follow them. 'Strictly girls only. But don't look so forlorn, I'll turn away while you kiss your long-lost fiancée goodnight.'

Renata laughed. Colin laughed. So Junia laughed. She moved to Colin's arms, felt him embrace, then release her, then saw him go. She turned to Renata to find that in spite of what she had said, she had watched. But the smile she gave Junia was a bright one.

'Pretty,' she said. 'I love lovers.' Another small laugh. 'Now follow me, the lighting is poor here, we need to conserve it.'

'Yes,' said Junia a little unevenly, obeying the girl, but the unevenness was not because of the poor lighting, not because of Renata's scrutiny, it was because of what Renata had said. 'I love lovers.' For that was what we were *not* just now, Junia was thinking. Just as in Colin's pre-fab, something hadn't been there.

She wondered if Renata had noticed. She seemed a very cool, very perceptive person. She wondered if that was why Renata had not turned away ... had seen there had been no call to turn in the lightness of Colin's kiss, in Junia's own light embrace back.

'Here we are!' Renata called.

It was a plain but sufficient room, sufficiently furnished. It had its own wash-basin, but the bath, Renata explained, was along the passage.

'Really a private bath,' she gloated, 'there are no other digs down this end, so I ... we now ... have the bathroom to ourselves.'

'I'm sorry about that, Renata, I mean I'm sorry about intruding into your exclusiveness like this.'

'Only woman in the project?' asked Renata, then shrugged. 'Don't give it a second thought, for the men certainly don't.'

'That I can't believe, you're too beautiful. But I think I can follow ... well, in a way. As the big boss's fiancée you would naturally be taboo.' Junia glanced meaningly at Renata's ring, a very lovely, very expensive-looking opal.

'As the boss's——' Renata began to echo, then she stopped herself to nod instead. 'I suppose so,' she said. 'All the same, they're not a particularly prepossessing lot.'

'Project workers generally have one thing on their mind.'

'Yes, build up a healthy bank balance, then depart. Frankly, Junia, it's been deadly boring here, that is it would have been but for——'

'For your Mr Kemble,' smiled Junia, 'for your fiancé.'

'... Yes. But even then—I mean, Karl is away such a lot. He's one of those annoying people who won't give out minor jobs, won't trust anyone on lesser explorations. He insists on doing them all himself.'

'I think he would be thorough,' Junia commented.

'Oh, yes, Karl is thorough. Well, this is your room, dear, and I'm next door. Meals are on at all hours and follow the hatch system. You know, you go to a wretched little window and say what you want, then bear it away to some miserable corner.'

'But you needn't, surely,' objected Junia. 'Couldn't you eat with some of the others?'

'If I wanted to. I don't. Also' ... a pause ... 'if they wanted you.' Another pause. 'But they don't.'

Junia barely heard her. Her eyes, roving round the room again, had noticed several things that had not struck her when she first had come in—a calendar on the wall, a small ornament, magazines by the bed.

'Renata,' she objected, 'I do believe you've given me your room.'

A split second, not even that, flashed past, then Renata said: 'Well, yes, I did, but I didn't want you to know. You see, I remember how it feels to come into a room with nothing in it, I mean nothing additional, nothing personal, so——'

'Oh, you are kind, Renata, but it won't do, of course. I'm going into the genuinely vacant room at once.'

'No. No, Junia, I would be most hurt. I want you in this room. You can't disappoint me.' Renata sounded quite concerned.

'Well, I suppose not if you feel like that about it.'

'I do,' Renata assured her.

'But why, Renata? Why all this trouble?'

'I told you—I've been through it, through being a new-chum, and it's a dismal business. Besides, it was no trouble changing round.'

'You had to pack your bags in that short time.' Junia, remembering how long it took her to pack one bag, was full of wonder that anyone could have removed their things so quickly.

'It was nothing. Colin helped me.—About Colin, Junia. I hope you haven't been getting any wrong ideas.'

'What do you mean—wrong ideas?'

'Colin, not being attached to the project, being an independent resident, has had rather a rough time, I think. I'm not blaming anyone, and particularly not

63

Karl, but I can't bring myself to treat him as the others have.'

'As you also have been treated?'

'Oh, no,' Renata said rather too quickly. 'No, I wouldn't like you to get that impression, the impression that we are two of a sort, your fiancé and I. It's simply that I felt sorry for Colin. I have that kind of nature.'

'Then I'm glad for Colin,' said Junia warmly, 'and glad at this moment most of all for myself for being given the best room, for I feel it *is* the best, Renata.'

'Think nothing of it,' assured Renata. 'I'll leave you now, you'll be tired and ready for a proper bed, not a sleeping bag. The bathroom's up the passage, dear. Knock on the wall any time that you need company or a cup of coffee. And *welcome*, Junia.' With that Renata went gracefully out of the room.

Having no bag to unpack ... she would speak to Renata about that tomorrow ... Junia decided to have the luxury of a bath, and then go to bed.

She went along the passage in her jeans, and lay blissfully in the hot water, smiling at the memory of her last 'bathtub', a caught-up lagoon that had mirrored back what she had considered a very unbeautiful countenance but Karl had called ... facetiously? ... a morning star. He had said tonight he might show her a western morning star tomorrow, but ... and a grin that turned to a grimace as Junia realised distastefully she would have to put on her dusty jeans to get back to her room ... he would come to the wrong digs. He would not know that Renata had moved. How extraordinarily kind it had been of Renata to shift out like that.—Also, how extraordinarily odd for someone else's fiancé to suggest such a thing as a morning star.

But she did not linger on that.

Scuttling back with the intention of rinsing her shirt and jeans in the wash-basin and letting them dry overnight, Junia slowed a little as she passed Renata's new room, the room that ordinarily would have been hers. No, it was not as large, she judged, not as good, but the layout of the hostel was such that Renata had only to come out of her door, then swing into a narrow downward flight of steps to leave the building. They could almost have comprised *her* stairs. Also, anyone entering could have come this handy way, too, instead of the front door and the two long halls.

Forgetting it at once, Junia regained her room, washed tomorrow's attire and hung it out of the window.

She was tired now, tired enough to sink into bed. She flopped thankfully, glad she was no longer confined to a sleeping bag, even a large one. She missed the stars, though, the blobs of stars and the melon of a moon. She felt herself beginning to drift. She was out in the bush again, all the stirrings and whirrings soothing her once more, the wood pigeons, the scrub turkeys, the herby leaves, the aromatic twigs.

... No, there was *no* herby smell, *no* aroma, *no* tang. There was, and forgetting her sleepiness Junia sat up for a moment, that faint sweetness again. That pale drift of——

Yes, it was jasmine.

CHAPTER FIVE

WHEN Junia woke the next morning the jeans and shirt hanging out of the window were bone dry. She supposed that up here drying clothes would never be a problem, and after splashing her face in the corner basin she climbed into her gear, glad that denim looked equally fresh unironed as ironed. A comb through her hair and some lipstick completed her make-up, compulsorily completed it, for she had nothing else to add. She looked at her watch and decided that Renata should be awake, went out to her door and gave a quiet tap.

When the tap was unanswered, she tapped louder and longer, and at length accepted the fact that though Renata might look a lotus flower, she evidently was not. She had obviously breakfasted already and could even be hard at work. Feeling a failure even this early in the piece, Junia hung around until the distant aroma of coffee enticed her along the passage from which Karl Kemble had appeared last night.

She passed a bar ... empty ... on the way, a smoking room, a billiard and games room, a library and writing room, a commonroom, all also empty, and at one end of the commonroom a mess fixed in the hatch system, as Renata had described. There was no one in the mess, no one visible behind the hatch, but there were big urns of coffee waiting, big pots of tea plus milk, sugar and mugs on the table beside the hatch, so Junia gratefully filled up a mug and made for the furthest table.

She was just taking a welcome gulp when she saw that another customer had arrived. It was Karl Kemble, and he did not go to the hatch, he shouted instead: 'I'm here, Joe,' and went to sit down. He did not do it, though, halfway there he noticed Junia, and came across to the corner table.

'Special order?' were his first words as he looked down at her coffee and nothing else. 'You're waiting?'

'Oh, no, I only wanted this.'

'I bet you did,' he grinned disbelievingly, 'you certainly managed to stow away more out there.' He nodded to a window and she knew what he meant.

'Fresh air, I expect,' she proffered.

'I don't believe it, I believe you were too shy to go to the hatch and tell Joe what you wanted.'

'I have what I want.'

'But not what I want you to want. Hi, Joe!' He had a very loud ringing voice. 'Make that twice!'

'Yes, boss,' Joe came back, though Joe himself did not appear.

'You shouldn't have bothered,' Junia objected. 'It was my own fault, I must have overslept. Renata was gone by the time I tapped on her door.'

'Oh, yes, she's an early riser.'

'Yet she looks so——'

'Yes,' he said again. 'So.' There was a moment of silence, broken by Joe putting down two plates at the window shelf, then disappearing again before Junia could see him. 'Come,' Karl Kemble ordered, 'Joe performs the miracles but delivers them only to the servery, the next step is ours.'

'Yes,' Junia said.

She followed Karl's example of taking up a tin tray and adding the necessary tools, then putting the plate on the tray and bearing it back to the table.

'It's a terrible lot,' Junia demurred of her plate, 'I mean a terrible lot for breakfast.' There was steak, eggs, onions, potatoes, the whole bit.

'It's a terrible lot of work,' Karl Kemble shrugged, 'the men here have to be well stoked for the toil I ask of them.'

'But I'm not a man, and I'm not toiling at all, let alone toiling terribly hard,' Junia pointed out.

'Pass the tomato sauce, less chatter, get on with it,' he replied.

She did . . . resentfully at first, then with an appetite she must have learned in the bush, for in Sydney she had been strictly a tea and toast girl.

'Sleep well?' Already he had finished the first part and was now drinking coffee and munching toast and jam.

'Yes. It's an excellent bed. I really must thank Renata for being so kind as to give up her own room for me.'

'Did she?' he asked.

'She moved out and took the end room,' Junia shrugged.

'Nearer to the small flight of steps,' he shrugged. 'A very handy thing, a very convenient set of stairs.'

'But she was near before.'

'Yes, but she would have had to pass your door had she let you have the empty room near the steps.'

'I don't understand.'

'Nothing to understand,' he shrugged . . . but his eyes were narrowed, Junia noticed.

'Mr Kemble, we will have to discuss payment to you,' she said.

'For your board?'

'Yes. Oh, I know you offered me this accommodation, but I must still pay.'

He agreed coolly. 'Of course you'll pay. But no talk

68

now, please, I've enough on my plate, and I reckon you must have, too.'

'Yes, but I would feel easier——'

'Then feel uneasy. As soon as I finish this I'm out on the field today. You can fill in your time mooching around, visiting your chap.'

'Of course.' Junia did not realise how eagerly she said that until he drawled:

'No laggard lover, anyway, on *your* side, eh?'

She flushed. She had burst it out, she knew, but it had been only to break up something—what, she could not have said.

After a while he warned her that there would be few places for her to visit apart from Colin's house. 'Once away from this street and you're in the wilderness again, *forbidden* wilderness.'

'What?'

'Well, not all of it, but what I consider should be kept quiet just now. There you *can't* go.'

'How will I know? Do you have guards? Do you have a sign Keep Out? Do you have savage dogs? An electric alarm?'

'I have rows of red flags, madam, indicating—Well, indicating will do for you at present. Where you find those red flags, you stop, then turn back.'

'I see.'

'Just make sure you do.'

He was getting up, wiping a paper napkin impatiently over his mouth.

'Mr Kemble, is there a store?' Junia asked.

'Yes. Kind of.'

'How kind of?'

'Writing tablets, pins, girly magazines with centre folds of the mate of the month (female persuasion, naturally) toothpaste, women's underthings to send back as presents——'

'Oh, good,' inserted Junia hopefully of that last, 'then face cream, perhaps?'

'No. Zinc cream for sunburn. Will that do?'

Dolefully Junia said it would have to do.

'Women's shirts?' she asked. 'I mean you said you had underthings.'

'By that I meant knickers with roses,' he said without a ghost of a smile, '*under* things. If you want over things you better look for small men's.'

'Then you do employ small men?' Junia looked up at him and his vast height with distinct hate. Him and his knickers with roses!

'We're only interested in a man's output, not his height and bulk,' Karl Kemble replied blandly. 'The store is behind the bar. You go through, help yourself, then pay George the barman. Anything else?'

'Nothing else ... but you will tell me how much I shall be indebted to you?'

'Be assured of that.' By the time the last word left his lips Karl Kemble was out of the mess door and striding down the passage.

Junia followed more slowly, hoping to catch the eye of the elusive cook behind the hatch, thank him, then ask what times the other meals were served.

Joe appeared, and Junia put on her best smile, which she had been told ... and apart from Colin and even Ned at Far-Flung ... was a smile worth smiling back at. 'You smile with your eyes, too,' someone had said, 'and it really gets to a fellow. Most smiles just brush over.'

She felt she was smiling and meaning it now, but she struck a blank in Joe. There was no smile back.

Joe grunted : 'Meals are on all day. Just shout your order through the hatch,' then disappeared.

'Thank you,' Junia said to nobody in a dampened voice.

She found the canteen she had passed before, still empty, but behind the bar this time there was a man polishing glasses. She went up to him and tried out her smile, though a little uncertainly now.

To say the least the smile back was just as uncertain. No, that was being magnanimous, Junia thought, more than uncertain it was downright unfriendly. What was wrong up here? Was every man a woman-hater?

'I was told the store was behind here,' she said.

The bartender still polished.

'Told by Mr Kemble,' Junia added in a louder voice.

At once she got service.

'Yes, go through the door. Everything we've got for sale is laid out. There's no attendant. Whatever you fancy you bring in to me, and I'll tell you the price.'

That suited Junia. She didn't want male service for the underwear she needed, and it would have to be male service, for Renata was the only female here. But what didn't suit her was the man's back turned on her at once as though ... well, as though she was an enemy. She had visited a friend working in a hydro project once and been envious over the fuss Miranda had had made over her. Here it was fuss in reverse.

Well, whether he liked it or not, she had to buy clothes. She crossed beyond the bar and pushed open a door.

She had not known what she had expected. Not the same as at Savage Gully, she supposed, for there the workers had had their own domestic pre-fabs, with their wives in them to cook for them, so there had been food supplies on sale. There had been bacon hanging from the rafters, tins of beans and strawberry jam. But here they ate all they wanted in the eating room, so there was no need for hanging bacons, beans and strawberry jam. It took away the rather muddled appeal, Junia thought, looking around at piles of boxes, some with lids open, some with lids askew and some still intact.

She began at the end of the big bench, and was glad to find that at least the contents were labelled.

The goods were not much to her liking, though. Whoever had ordered the fancy boxes of lingerie had had a very limited colour range, either that or he had believed in thinking pink. All the sets ... knickers with roses, Karl Kemble had said ... were very pink and very awash with lace. Still, a beggar could not be a chooser. Junia took up two of the plainer designs. They were the only female attire offering, obviously by the ribboned presentation intended for gifts for sending home, as he, Karl Kemble, had said. There were no jeans, as she had hoped, and no tops.

Well, it looked as if it would have to be Small Men, if possible Small Small Men.

No, Junia discovered ten minutes later, there might be some small men here, but certainly no small small. Thank goodness looseness was the fashion today. She picked out three shirts, then, making sure the bartender was still polishing glasses, though there was little likelihood of his putting his disapproving face round the door, she pulled out a pair of small drill pants and quickly tried them on. Not perfect by any means ... men's shapes were undoubtedly different from women's ... but the pants zipped and looked fairly neat.

Pleased with her discoveries, she tried for cosmetics. Perhaps some had been included also to send south for gifts. But except for zinc cream, as Karl Kemble also had said, Junia could find nothing, so she finished her purchases with a slab of chocolate, then went back to the bar.

The bartender tallied them up and accepted her money without comment; Junia had at least expected a grunt over the drill pants. He gave back the change and Junia went out. A cheerful bunch, I must say, she remarked to herself, the boss, the cook, the bartender; I wonder how the rest will react? The dourness made her want to run down to Colin in the warm anticipation of being treated like a human being, but instead, after depositing her purchases in her room, she walked, not raced, down the side steps that Karl Kemble had shrugged over and called 'handy' ... 'convenient' ... then over the rough road to the house at the very end.

This morning she could see in the bright daylight, not just guess in the dark plush of the night, and she looked around her with interest. Not much to look at, as the boss had warned, but still interesting in a strange way, beautiful in a strange way. The beauty of line and shape entirely without adornment. With colour to call upon when it wanted it there was no need for adornment.

The street ... not a street, not even a road, just a track that had grown ... was rough with rocks and hazardous with holes. There was a line of pre-fabs on the opposite side to the hostel, by the look of them taken over now for offices, leaving the building this side exclusively for communal living. Then there was a gap in the line of pre-fabs, then after that break, standing on its own, Colin's abode. The break gave Junia the opportunity to gaze beyond the 'town' of Far-Off, and what she saw proved the wilderness that Kemble had said, but such a lovely wilderness that she caught her breath and halted. The earth had been shattered in many places from explosives as 'signs' were followed up, and the piled-high waste shone blood-red in the brilliant sunshine. Because ore was present, the terrain

73

took on a purple haze, one of the beautiful things that iron ore achieves, but it was not ore that was being pursued in that country further out, country stretching to old ochre hills, it was something obviously more important, because it was marked with red geologist's flags, wherever the ground was not covered with red Sturt Pea, it gleamed electric blue from the west's eternal Salvation Jane.

'Junia! For heaven's sake!'

With a little start Junia realised she must have been standing there gazing, gazing long enough to irritate Colin, for his reproof came sharply across at her from his house.

'I'm sorry.' She had come up to him now. 'It was so lovely.'

'People will think you're sizing it up, you silly girl.'

'What on earth are you talking about, Colin? Sizing what up? I was just admiring it.'

'Or its possible potential?'

'Its what?' she questioned.

'Just come in, Junia, and let me close the door.'

Junia obeyed, her confusion ... and a certain little indignation ... momentarily diverted by that pale scent again, that whiff of jasmine. Colin *must* have changed his cologne.

By the time he crossed from the door to her, Colin was in a better mood. He took her in his arms and kissed her.

'Sorry, sweet, but this place does get one on edge.'

'Then you must leave it, of course.' Junia hoped he did not hear a faint note of regret in her voice; she had loved everything about Far-Off at once, had even had instant thoughts about staying here, making it her place.

74

'Oh, I will, have no second thoughts about that, but not until I finish what I'm doing.'

'And what is that, Colin? You never told me last night.'

'Sit down. Coffee?'

'I had some in the canteen.'—And steak and eggs and all the trimmings, Junia could have added.

'Renata took you?' He spoke in surprise. 'She never mentioned it.'

'*Renata* never mentioned it?'

At once Colin came in smoothly: 'I saw her on her way to her office ... that string of pre-fabs up further is used for the secretarial, managerial, mineralogy, physics, biochemistry and what-have-you departments, not for housing. Only sleeping, eating and drinking are done at the hostel.'

'Yes,' said Junia a little wonderingly. She had gathered such a conclusion on her way down to Colin's, but Colin's lone four rooms by two was certainly not on the track to Renata's office.

As though he read her thoughts, Colin said briskly: 'I jog every morning. A man needs excercise out here, especially bent over a desk all day. Renata doesn't take breakfast, she prefers to start early to defeat the heat. She probably thought you would sleep in so didn't disturb you. I saw her then.'

Junia nodded. It was unimportant, anyhow, she thought, that already this early they had met.

'You haven't told me about your work, Colin,' she said. 'I know you've been doing articles for mining magazines, but frankly I've never seen any.'

'You'd only get the Sydney editions.' Colin rather mumbled it.

'I got none, as a matter of fact,' smiled Junia, 'mineral outputs and such are not a woman's cup of tea.

But I have turned over pages at the bookstall during lunch break and sneaked a free read. I never ever saw your name.'

'You could have missed it, Junia, but I've been featured, how otherwise am I existing?' He glanced significantly around him.

'And existing handsomely,' Junia nodded.

'Also,' went on Colin, 'I've been on something else, something much bigger.'

'What's that, Colin?'

'Junia, I'm writing a book.'

'On all this?' Junia spread her hands to embrace the unit and beyond the unit.

'Yes.'

'But how wonderful!' Junia felt very proud of him.

'I've even found a publisher and had an advance already,' Colin told her. 'So that answers your question, doesn't it, as to what I've been doing and how I can afford to do it.'

'I didn't mean it quite that baldly,' Junia regretted. 'I'm terribly pleased for you. Particularly when—well——'

'Yes, Junia?'

'When you weren't ever very good on such things,' said Junia apologetically. 'Oh, you knew what you wanted to say, Colin, but you couldn't express it, couldn't express yourself.'

'I thought I gave you graphic accounts.'

... 'Probably take from a book.' ... That had been Karl Kemble, and Junia remembered it now.

'You never gave me what I wanted most,' she reproached gently, 'in your letters.'

'Sorry, dearest, but I've always clammed up when it got round to fiction.'

'Fiction?' she queried.

76

'You know what I mean, Junia. But give me facts ... And facts are what I'm dealing with now, Junia, and yes, I must say it, dealing damn well. So there's your Colin for you. Working harder than I think you believed Colin could, getting ready for the day he can escape.'

'Escape?'

'From here.' Colin had flushed now. 'From what do you think I wanted to escape?'

'Me? Marriage?' Junia laughed.

'Oh, don't be silly, darling, as though I could ever want that! No, it's this place that bugs me. I can't get away quick enough.'

'Then, Colin, let's both leave at once.' It hurt her to say that, but she felt it was the best. She was surprised by Colin's instant denial.

'By what?' he demanded. 'I have no car, and even if I had it would have to be a powerful one, something like Kemble's four-wheel drives, to get us out. No, I'm stuck here for a while. Anyway, I couldn't go yet.'

'Why?'

'My book,' Colin reminded her a little truculently.

'Couldn't you write up your notes, get away by the supply van or—or something, then finish the book in Sydney?'

'It's a book that must be finished *here*, Junia.'

'Local colour?' Junia said that wryly; she had never known a book dealing in facts that needed local colour. Now, if Colin was writing imaginatively, bringing in, for instance, that view through his window of a shaggy bark tree hung with a swaying water bag ...

'You're being astringent, Junia,' Colin complained. 'The old Junia I knew was never like that.'

'I'm sorry, Colin, I know I'm being difficult. But there's an atmosphere somehow——'

77

'Atmosphere?' Colin picked it up quickly.

'I—I feel I'm not wanted here.'

'My dearest!'

'No, not you.' But somewhere deep—and dismayed —in her, Junia knew she could have said instead: 'Others as well as you.' She wondered *why* she was feeling like this, actually Colin had given her no cause.

'Then who?' Colin was demanding urgently on her behalf.

She told him.

'The mess this morning ... Joe was—well—— Then the shop afterwards ... Both men so unco-operative. So—well, near-suspicious. Definitely not wanting me.'

'But *I* want you, Junia.'

Colin had crossed to her, and his arms around her were tight and possessive. They cut out everything; the room, the window, the distance beyond the window with that solitary bark tree waving a water bag. But they could not cut out that scent, that faint drift of jasmine where instead there should have been the tang of the bush, or, closer, Colin's cologne, mint cologne.

They could not cancel an odd, unable-to-be-explained wonder in Junia's mind. Almost, she felt, as though, in spite of Colin's closeness, something ... someone ... stood between.

CHAPTER SIX

It was quite a few moments before Junia realised that someone *was* standing close. Not between them, of course, but certainly very near them. She felt it first in Colin's barely discernible but instinctive withdrawal from her, followed soon after by the disengaging of his arms. A glimpse of Renata standing watching them came at the same time as Renata's teasing voice.

'Oh, you lovers!' Renata called.

There was a smile in her voice, but it was not one of those smiles that Junia had been pleased to be told she produced. It did not reach Renata's dark eyes and it only brushed her mouth. At once, as though she realised this, Renata said quickly:

'Alas, I'm a grass widow, I envy you two so much I've gone and let it show.'

'Does Mr Kemble have to leave you often, Renata?' Junia, completely disengaged now, asked the girl sympathetically.

'Yes. That's the wretched west for you.' Renata shrugged. 'I saw you pass my office door, Junia, and signalled you. But you' ... another smile ... 'were so anxious to find Colin you never noticed.'

'Actually I was looking at the country ... it's wonderful country ... but I'm afraid Colin was annoyed with me. He thought someone might see me and think I was sizing it up, whatever he means by that.'

'Junia, don't let's bore Renata with domestic arguments,' came in Colin at once, but the lovely dark girl brushed his words aside.

'Colin was right, poor dear,' she told Junia ruefully. 'Like all these exploratory places everyone is suspect. You have no idea of the entanglements of the west.'

'It sounds exciting,' commented Junia.

'It's disgusting. For example, when I saw how the project was treating Colin simply because he was an outsider, I was quite enraged. However, that, as I said, is the west.'

'So you comforted him, Renata?'

There was the quickest exchange of glances between the girl and the man, so brief it might not have been an encounter at all, only Junia's imagination.

'Oh, no,' said Renata, 'I would never do that, Junia, but I also would not ignore him, as some of the men here have ignored him.'

'Including Mr Kemble?'

'Big Brother is always civil,' came in Colin, civil himself on this occasion, 'but——'

'But Joe and George?' suggested Junia with a grin.

'So you've already experienced them, too.' Renata and Colin spoke almost together.

'Yes, I have,' sighed Junia. 'What is it? I thought they might be woman-haters, but if Colin is included——'

'They're simply old hands,' offered Renata in explanation, 'and no one resents newcomers like the oldies. But you're right, too, about women. *I* am barely tolerated.'

'Even though you're the boss's fiancée?'

There was a brief pause. Then: 'Yes,' Renata said.

'I see now why you eat away from the hostel,' Junia sympathised.

'But I don't. I just don't take breakfast, that's why you didn't see me this morning. I *have* to eat my meals at the dining room. There's nowhere else to go. Even Colin here has to swallow his pride and take a plate from the servery hatch.'

'Do you, Colin?' asked Junia, surprised.

'Well, dear, there's no shops from which to buy supplies, so what else? I pay Kemble, of course.'

'Of course.' Junia remembered her own business talk with the boss today, recalled that he had said the same two words after she had told him she would pay him. He had said coolly:

'Of course.'

'It was uncomfortable for me,' related Colin plaintively, 'that first day. I felt like a Philistine. But Renata took pity on me, thank goodness, and now she eats at the same table.'

'And Mr Kemble?'

'He eats there, too, when he's present,' said Colin.

'Which is not often,' added Renata.

'Then with me it will be an uncomfortable four whenever Mr Kemble does deign.' Junia could not hide a grin.

'But,' said Colin feelingly, 'there'll be three on our side to make it easier.'

Junia smiled. She could not accept that. 'Oh, Colin, don't be silly, a fiancée is always on the side of her fiancé.'

Again, almost imperceptibly yet *there*, there was that brief exchange of glances.

Renata broke a silence. She said a little hurriedly: 'Colin has just said there are no shops, but I think you've discovered one shop, Junia.'

Junia laughed, glancing down at the chocolate in her pocket, its silver top showing above the denim of her jeans.

'This was only one of my purchases from the dour

81

George,' she related. 'I bought shirts, a pair of drill pants, a set of lingerie' ... almost she had said knickers with roses ... 'and since there was nothing else, then nothing else.'

'What was it you wanted?' asked Renata helpfully. 'Oh, I know you didn't want pink lingerie frothing with lace, but it's all that's ever offering. But—anything else?'

'Face cream,' sighed Junia, 'that isn't zinc.'

'But my dear, I have plenty. Experience teaches you to bring plenty. This isn't my first remote assignment. You're very welcome to take what you need. You must pick out other things, too. We can't have you going around in a man's shirt and drills looking like one of Karl's "fellers",' Renata refused. She smiled at Colin. 'Agreed?'

'Agreed,' Colin said.

Renata now turned her attention from Junia to Colin. 'How is the book?' she asked.

... So Colin indeed was writing a book, was Junia's first thought. In spite of what he had told her, she had still doubted him, for Colin had never been a writer. Junia's second thought after that was: 'So he's told Renata, too.'

As quickly as she had read her before Renata said brightly: 'Actually I suggested the book, Junia, between doing his mining articles Colin was getting quite down in the dumps. It was the atmosphere here.'

'I can understand *that*,' Junia said feelingly.

'So I encouraged him to start a book, and now he has discovered all sorts of unknown talents.'

'Even snared a publisher who'll give him an advance,' admired Junia.

Again that quick exchange.

'I was glad to hear that,' Junia went on, 'I was beginning to wonder where his furniture came from. It's very good, isn't it?'

'And inexpensive,' Renata assured her. 'Colin bought it from a departing mining executive. It would cost the world to transport up here. Now, dear, unless Colin wants you particularly, do come up to the hostel and select your things. I work whatever hours I like, and as I started early I can spare the time. Back to work, Colin. Your fiancée says so.' She smiled promptingly at Junia to say so.

'Yes, I mustn't delay you,' Junia complied.

The two girls left the pre-fab and walked up the rough road again.

They did not go up the main steps, they used Kemble's 'handy' ... 'convenient' ... staircase. Junia opened her own door first and showed Renata her purchases.

'Poor pet,' sympathised Renata over the lacy lingerie, 'what southern company has been unloading its unwanted froth on the long-suffering north-west? No doubt Karl, on George's advice, simply wrote down for gift packs for the little woman back home, and this is what happened.'

'It looks wearable enough,' grinned Junia, 'and will certainly crush flat under the drill pants I also bought.'

'You shouldn't have,' said Renata, 'I could have fitted you out with slacks and shirt.'

'I'm right now, thank you, but I don't fancy moisturising with zinc cream.'

'Then I can help you there at least, I have a big supply. Come and choose for yourself.'

Renata led the way to her room, at least her own room now, and it was not near so large or well-aspected as Junia's. Why *had* Renata been so kind? Because she simply was kind ... or because of handiness ... convenience? Now why had she thought that?

'There,' said Renata, and she displayed a supply of bottles and jars. 'This climate is hard on the skin, so I see to it that I never run out.'

'Then if I accept something you might run out.'

'I don't think so. I don't think I'll be here that long. I mean' ... quickly ... 'I'll be having a break in Sydney before that, so I can stock up again.'

'How long have you been up here, Renata?' asked Junia.

'Six—seven months.'

'Then you must have come almost at the same time as Colin.'

'Yes ... yes, I believe we did. Junia, take this bottle, too.'

Renata was now making coffee out of a jug plugged to a power point and from a jar of instant.

'I only go down to the eatery for necessary meals,' she explained. 'Do you mind black?'

'No, Renata. Thank you.'

The coffee poured into mugs and sugar produced, the two girls sat down on Renata's bed.

'How long do you plan to stay here, Junia?' Renata asked openly.

Her frankness pleased Junia. Renata had been very nice, very obliging, but she had seemed to withhold something. Her directness now helped Junia in her reply.

'When I came, I had no idea. All I wanted to do was see Colin, go on from there.'

'Of course.'

'I did think that perhaps I could stay here ... or that perhaps Colin would be ready to leave, only I can see now that it would be wrong to ask him to move in the middle of his book. So' ... Junia spread her hands ...

'as soon as it's convenient for Mr Kemble to take me out, I'll push off again and wait in Sydney for Colin.'

'No, don't go,' Renata said at once. 'It's lovely having another woman. It's like the end of a drought in a way,' she smiled.

'That's very kind of you, Renata, but how could I stop? I did have a hazy picture of looking around the place, exploring, making a few sketches, painting, for I like to dabble at times, but—well, it isn't that sort of background, is it? You have to have a reason to be here, a reason to move around, and I've none at all.'

'You *could* have,' insinuated Renata.

'You mean cook for Colin to save him coming up here for meals? But there are no shops, no supplies.'

'You could—work here.'

'Work here? But there's no opening.'

'Have you tried?' asked Renata.

'No, but I just gathered there wasn't, that you handled that need.'

'I could do with help,' Renata said.

Junia positively glowed. 'It would be wonderful,' she agreed, 'it would be a solution, but how could I? I mean, you can't barge your way in.'

'You can ask.'

'It might sound as if I was trying to undermine you.'

'Look, Junia,' said Renata, 'my leave is coming up fairly soon, and I'm sure Karl would agree that it would be better to have my work done than piled up waiting for my return.'

'I suppose so, but—what about Colin?'

'Colin?'

'Well—I'm not quite sure if Colin wants me here,' Junia said with the same frankness that Renata had adopted.

Renata smiled, shook her head emphatically and

touched Junia's hand. 'What a funny idea, the poor man has literally been pining for you. Look, Junia, I must tell you something,' she went on. 'Colin and I were talking together *before* I walked down to his house just now and spoiled a romantic moment.'

'Yes, I know, he told me he had seen you as he jogged by your office.'

'And you promptly thought: "What a lie!" ... Well, didn't you?'

'Yes, I did,' Junia grinned at Renata. 'Colin was never one for exercise.'

'Well, it was a lie,' Renata admitted. 'I'd come down to confer with him. No, not about the book, but about you.'

'Me?'

'Yes.'

'But why didn't Colin say so?'

'My dear, you two have been away from each other for months, he could have thought you would be—hurt.'

'Hurt?' questioned Junia.

'Hurt that he had another woman in his house.'

Junia said a little curiously: 'Would you be hurt with your fiancé?'

'No.'

'Then——?'

'But Karl—well, Karl——' Renata began.

'Yes?'

'Karl is a very actual, factual person, Junia. I mean, holes in the ground are his *first* thoughts.'

'Yet you love him,' Junia pointed out.

'... Oh, yes.' If there was any hesitation, again it was barely that.

'Why did you need to confer with Colin concerning me, Renata?' asked Junia.

86

'It was the *keeping* you here that I had on my mind, Junia. I knew poor Colin would be driven silly with the same idea. Why the foolish boy didn't tell you how we discussed you I can only put down to a reluctance on Colin's part to ask you to do what would have to be done.'

'Have to be done?' echoed Junia.

'By you, if you're to stay.'

'It is?'

'A request to Karl for a job. Your own personal request.'

'But—but I couldn't do that,' Junia protested, 'it—it would be an imposition on my part. I have no right.'

'But you'd like to stay?'

'Oh, yes.'

'Then?'

'Then nothing, Renata, because I doubt if I could even if I did decide to. No, I think words would fail me.'

'But Colin certainly couldn't, not in his unpopular role.'

'No,' agreed Junia. She asked tentatively: 'Could you?'

'No. *No*. No, it would have to come from you. If I asked Karl would immediately say the job was too much for me and pack me off south.'

'But you said you were going, anyway.'

'For a break,' Renata reminded her. She waited a moment. 'Karl is—well, a difficult customer, even though we're——' She smiled winningly and glanced down to her left hand. 'You have to tread carefully with him, Junia. If I asked outright I'd do more damage than good. That's my Karl. He's a black and white man, I always say, no shades of grey at all. No, *you*

would have to do the asking. That is' ... shrewdly ...
'if you're really interested.'

'Oh, I am, Renata, I'm very interested.'

'Then give it a try. He can't eat you. Only——'

'Yes?'

'Don't bring me in, Junia. I don't need to remind
you not to bring in Colin.'

'No, you don't, and I wouldn't mention you either
if I did pluck up the courage.'

'Pluck it up, Junia.'

'I—I think I might try. And Renata——'

'Yes, Junia?'

'Thank you for your thoughtfulness. It seems you
never stop doing things for me.'

'Well,' Renata smiled, 'perhaps one day you'll do
something for me.'

'Oh, I will!'

'I'll take you up on that. My goodness, I'd better
get back to the office and put in another hour before
lunch. I'll see you in the eatery, Junia ... Colin, too ...
even Karl if he's in from the field. Quite a bright table,'
Renata laughed wryly. 'But don't,' she advised, 'burst
your request on Karl there and then. Pick the right
moment. Which should be' ... she smiled knowingly
... 'this afternoon. I heard Karl ordering his Cherokee
to be fuelled. I reckon he's going to give you a flip
around.'

'I didn't know there was a plane,' said Junia.

'Just a small one for emergencies. It would be no
use for carting in supplies.'

'And why should you think Mr Kemble would take
me? He heartily disapproves of me.'

'But he loves this land. His love of this land comes
before anything else.' A resentful shadow crossed Renata's face. 'He's so proud of it he would have to show

it to you even if he despised you, even, too, if you declined and he had to carry you kicking to the plane to take you.'

'I wouldn't be kicking, I'd love to see it.'

'And slip in your request at the appropriate moment?'

'If you think it would be the appropriate moment.'

'It would be, Junia. It would be the only moment. You could look entranced——'

'I probably would be,' Junia agreed.

'And go on from there.'

'It sounds—well, coldblooded.'

'But then Karl is coldblooded. No—no, I don't mean that, of course, I mean he would respect you asking at such a wonderful time.'

'He would?' said Junia doubtfully.

'Believe me, dear. But lunch first ... after I write several important letters for the big boss. See you, Junia dear, and hoping to see you lots more. Let's keep our fingers crossed on that.' Renata held up her crossed fingers, smiled again, then went out and down the convenient steps.

Junia went to her own room.

Around noon she strolled down the corridor to the mess again. This time the rooms were alive. There were men in the writing room, library, bar. All of them glanced up as Junia went past, then all of them looked down once more. What *was* this place?

Junia would gladly have slunk back, gone without the meal, only she had told Renata she would see her here, and, looking round the corner of the eatery, Renata already was esconced. She saw Junia at once and beckoned her over. Junia had hardly sat down before Colin joined them.

From then on the room filled quickly ... and emptied

quickly. The men were fast eaters and were not anxious to linger over the meal. Not one of them glanced to the table in the corner.

When Karl Kemble came in, as Renata had anticipated he might, he was greeted on all sides, but still no one glanced to the table at which Karl seated himself.

The big boss nodded briefly to Colin, gave a mock salute to his fiancée, then a deliberately ironic bow to Junia.

'How is our guest amusing herself?'

'The morning flew,' Junia assured him.

'So will the food if we don't queue up.' Karl Kemble rose. 'As I told you earlier, Miss West, Joe performs the miracles, then leaves the rest to us. What's on?'

'Haricot steak,' read Junia from a piece of blackboard.

'I'll skip that,' Renata said.

Karl Kemble took no notice of his fiancée's likes, or rather dislikes.

'*You* won't.' He was looking remindingly at Junia.

Angry at him but not knowing what to say, and anyway she liked haricot steak, Junia followed him and took up a tray. She noticed that Colin, too, was 'skipping', but if Karl noticed, he said nothing.

They came back to the table, and there followed one of the most uncomfortable meals Junia had ever eaten. The food was good, project food perhaps, with that necessary large quantity taste, but good. Renata got up and brought coffee and rolls to the table and she and Colin ate these. Afterwards she fetched sweets.

Still Karl paid no notice. He ate silently, so the others did, too. Not until he had finished did he speak. Then he said : 'Thank you all for the spirited conversation, it makes for good digestion. Miss West' ... turning to Junia ... 'you said just now that the morning flew.'

'Yes.' Almost Junia answered, as she had on the track: 'Yes, Boss.'

'This afternoon *you* will fly. I'm flipping you round in the crate for you to see where you are.'

'By the crate you mean——' Junia did not dare meet Renata's eyes because of the laughter bubbling up in her and the I-told-you-so laughter she anticipated in Renata, but had she looked she would have been surprised, for there was no laughter.

'I fly a small craft.' Kemble spoke coolly. 'A two-seater. One seat for our visitor.' He nodded to Junia. 'One for myself as pilot. I'll see you in the front ... the main front, not the side steps ... in five minutes.' The same as at breakfast this morning his last words were spoken as he went through the door.

Junia looked after him, not knowing whether to be angered or amused. What an arrogant, what a self-sufficient man! By the time she turned and looked at Renata, Renata was smiling smoothly and saying: 'See, Junia, just as I said. My fiancée is obsessed.'

'With this country?'

'Yes.'

'Well, if *you* don't mind——'

'My dear, if I minded it would still make no difference, you'd still have to see this wretched terrain.'

'Is it to you, Renata? Is it wretched?'

Renata went to answer, then she hesitated shrewdly. 'No—no, of course not. I just get annoyed sometimes at the way Karl takes everything and everybody in his stride. Except that he's Karl and my—fiancé' ... again there was that slightest of hesitations ... 'I would say he was a positive roughrider. But I won't say it.' A charming smile and a significant glance down at her

91

left hand, third finger. 'Naturally. Now you get out and meet him, Junia, and don't forget——' Her eyes flicked a message and Junia nodded.

She went out of the mess and down to her room.

She did not change her clothes—he would not notice, anyway. She made do with a hair-comb and a trace of lipstick and went back again.

However, she was wrong about her gear. Karl Kemble did notice. He had his jeep drawn up at the steps, and he gave her a quick look.

'Still in the same jeans. I gave you five minutes in the hope you might emerge a woman. I have men all day, a woman would be a change.'

'You have Renata,' she reminded him.

'... My fiancée. Yes. But two would help.'

'I'm sorry, then, but your shop is not very accommodating when it comes to female apparel, and I shall still be wearing pants in the future.'

'But you did manage the——'

'The knickers with roses? Yes. Very pink, very awash with lace.'

'What else would a man ask?' he grinned.

'I'm a woman,' she pointed out coldly.

'In men's pants. All right, don't stand around, get in.'

Literally one minute from the project there could have been no project. The west took over.

Kemble drove furiously. Junia did not know how he could, for there was no track that she could see. There must have been some sort of indication, though, for unerringly, without any hesitation, he would turn at a stand of mulga, a thicket of bark trees, and presently he came out on a roughly cleared strip, and on the strip a small plane.

'Used only for flying out the sick or flipping up the

VIPs if we happen to be inflicted with them.' Karl was out of the jeep by now and nodding for Junia to get out, too.

'I'm not sick,' she said, 'so I must be a VIP.'

'Undoubtedly, since you're being flipped, but' ... a long look ... 'a VIP for whom? Whom are you important to, Miss West?'

'I don't understand you.'

'Don't you?' he said, and started walking to his craft. After a few seconds Junia walked, too. She climbed in beside him and did up her harness. The craft taxied and took off. It turned at once in a direction that Kemble called out to her was west.

'West, Miss West, until we reach the sea,' he said. 'Our own Indian Ocean.'

'That far!'

'Not far for the crow, and that's what we are now, crows.' He turned his attention to the controls.

Junia looked down eagerly. It was an entirely red land they flew over, but where the mining boom towns puctuated the scarlet miles there was that inevitable purple haze from the huge open-cut ore workings.

They left the mines for mountain country with deep gorges full of silver rock pools, rugged vastness, and, Karl called, fantastic wealth. They reached the coast, and there unrolled the Indian Ocean, surely the most blue of all oceans, but before the ocean there were unbelievable sounds, formed over millions of years ago from water and weather, and from down there the sea looked back at them in amazingly varied colours of red, brown, green and pastel pink.

They flew over railways formed to carry the ore to the wharves, these long, now tide-emptied wharves looking like skinny fingers pointing out to the cornflower blue of the endless ocean, then over salt farms shimmering in the sun.

Finally eastward again to the red country and home, away from the Indian Ocean and its one-time pearl luggers, for ore was the king now, and Karl Kemble flew his Cherokee proudly, acclaiming 'This is my country' in every movement of his strong mobile face, and Junia ... Junia was so enrapt she could not utter a word.

It was a pity it had to end, Junia thought afterwards, not just the magnificence of the scene but the unspoken rapport between them, between Karl Kemble and Junia West, as together they soared above and together they looked down.

But it did end ... through Junia.

They were on the home field again now, the crude little strip with last year's dead straw flower.

'Well?' Karl asked.

'It was—it was——'

'Yes?'

'I—I can't say,' she faltered.

'I know,' he nodded.

'Can I stay on here? Please can I stay?' She burst it out just like that.

'Would you like to?'

'Oh, yes, yes!' It was then Junia remembered Renata's prompting, and said: 'Can I work in your office?'

It sounded innocuous enough, it *was* innocuous ... well, as far as Junia was concerned it was innocuous. But the face he turned on her now was dull red with barely concealed anger and incredulity.

'So that's what you want?' he demanded.

'Yes.'

'You just don't want to stay here to be here, you want a job here?'

'Well, how otherwise can I stay? I mean, I haven't any money, and Colin——'

'Yes, Brent. Yes, I see.' Now his voice was dry.

'Mr Kemble, I don't understand you,' she faltered.

'Strange, I understand you.'

'Then you can see' ... eagerly ... 'how important it is to me, I mean how anxious I am to——'

'Oh, yes, I can see the importance and I can tell your anxiety.'

'Then?' she persisted.

'I'll think about it.' He was getting out of the craft. 'Meanwhile you can consider yourself Far-Off's guest for a week.'

'Oh, I couldn't!' Junia exclaimed.

'But you damn well will until I say.'

'Say?'

'Yes, madam, say: "You can work in the office" or say: "No, you can pack up and leave".'

'I have nothing to pack,' she said foolishly, 'but I do see.'

'Do you?' He was looking at her closely. 'I wouldn't know by your kind of face.'

'My kind of face?' she echoed.

'That morning star face, all credulity, all faith, all trust.'

'Perhaps I am like that.'

'You'd be the first then of your sex,' he said dryly.

'You don't like women,' she observed.

'Women have seen to that.'

'Yet you're engaged to Renata?'

'Yes' ... blandly ... 'the chap is engaged to Renata.'

'You speak as though you're speaking of someone else,' she said wonderingly.

'Oh, I'm speaking of me, be assured of that. Be

assured, too, that I'll think this over and give you ... and Brent ... my decision.'

'But it wasn't——' Almost Junia had said: 'It wasn't Colin, it was Renata.' She closed her lips. She mustn't say that to him.

Karl was walking to the jeep now, and she had to hurry to keep up with him.

'And I thought,' he was more thinking to himself than saying aloud, 'that you were looking down with the same eyes as I looked down.'

'I don't know about that,' Junia said humbly, angry with herself that she had approached him at the wrong time, though at the time it had not seemed wrong, 'I only know I saw magnificence.'

'The probability of staggering wealth is always magnificent.'

'But I wouldn't know that.' She looked at him in appeal.

'So it's the morning star again, is it? Credulity, faith and trust?'

'Mr Kemble, I——'

'Oh, be quiet, can't you? I can't take any more. I'll let you know.'

'In a week!'

'By the time we get back to base.'

Again they bounced over a track that did not exist, then as abruptly as they had left the project behind them, they reached it again. Karl pulled up, got out and came round to where Junia sat.

'The job's yours. You can start tomorrow—Renata will brief you. No thanks, please.'

He was up the hostel steps before Junia could call timidly but determinedly:

'Thank you, Mr Kemble.'

The boss did not respond.

CHAPTER SEVEN

WHEN Junia went along to the mess the next morning she crossed straight to the hatch and called out her wishes to Joe. There were more breakfasters present today, and she did not wish to be publicly reprimanded by Karl Kemble, should he appear, for reprimand, regardless of who listened or watched, that man certainly would. Anyway, and Junia smiled to herself, this country made her hungry. She took her plate from the servery, put it on a tray, added hot rolls and coffee, then sought the corner table once more.

No one took any notice of her. It appeared attention was only paid when the boss was there. It also seemed that this morning the boss either had breakfasted already, was still coming, or, like Renata, was skipping. That amused Junia. She could not imagine a large, earthy, powerful man like Karl Kemble skipping meals. She ate watching the swing doors, but when nothing happened, and nobody came, she finished her coffee, got up and went out. Still no focus of attention.

She wished Renata ate in the morning. Or that Colin came up. Though she had not let the silence spoil the meal, still a cheerful breakfast would have been much more enjoyable. But then joy was not what she was here for. She was here to work for her keep until such time as Colin was ready to leave.

Renata and Colin had been very pleased with her last night when she had told them the results of her employment request to Karl Kemble.

97

'So he said "Yes",' Renata had praised.

Junia had nodded.

'And you didn't——'

'No,' Junia had assured her.

'Then you've done very well, Junia dear. Well for me as well as for your Colin. *I* am happy I'm not losing you for woman reasons.' Renata had given Junia a warm girls-together look. '*Colin* is naturally happy because now you're legitimately here and so able to stay here.'

'The only thing,' Junia had submitted, 'was Mr Kemble's obvious lack of enthusiasm.'

There had been the quickest of glances between Renata and Colin.

'Only to be expected,' Renata had said at once. 'Karl is essentially a man who does the suggesting, is not suggested to. I've no doubt you suggesting you stay on as a clerk really surprised him, since he always sees to it that he gets in first.' She had made her voice sound affectionately, tolerantly critical, she had made it sound gently amused. A sort of 'I love him, but I still see his faults,' Junia had taken it. 'You are sure, dear,' she had repeated, 'that you made it your suggestion, your idea?'

'Sure.'

'Then you're a very clever girl.' A pause.—A prompting pause? Now why had she thought that?

Colin had come in at once: 'Yes, a very clever girl. My clever girl.' He had taken Junia's hand.

If a little nonplussing, it still had been very satisfying to Junia. She had solved her own problems as regarded staying on and at the same time pleased her fiancé and friend. If Karl Kemble had been less than enthusiastic, then he was in the minority. Though, thoughtfully, was a big boss ever in a minority?

Well, she would be in the minority if she did not turn up quite soon at the office, the minority, she suspected, who had been dismissed from here, for Karl Kemble, though obviously demanding, would be strictly fair, she judged, and would only discard after much thought. She did not want tardiness to begin any such thoughts, though, and since Renata began very early, thus setting an example, Junia went across the road at once.

She need not have hurried. Karl was not there. Nor at the moment was Renata. Junia was told this quite shortly by a man who emerged from an office marked: Facilities Construction Supervisor when she tapped on his door, which was the nearest door, to ask.

The Facilities Construction Supervisor ... whatever that was ... said no more but returned to his desk and his work.

There were other offices—Modification Draughtsman. Maintenance Planner. Hydraulics Engineer. Quantity Surveyor. Biochemist. They were all visible in their glass cages.

There was an office no larger and no more important-looking than the rest that simply ... deceptively simply? ... said K. Kemble. No Manager. No Executive. No Boss.

Junia had no need to check this office again, she had done it instinctively as soon as she had read the name by standing on tiptoe and blinking through the partition, but she did probe once more just to satisfy herself. No, he was not there. Out on the field, she supposed. She was disappointed. She was on time and she wanted someone to know it. The Facilities man would know it, so would the other occupants of the offices into which she had looked, but she doubted if it would be relayed. She sat disconsolately at Renata's desk, feeling very superfluous, wondering if there was any typing she could finish for her.

She leafed over a few pages, then became aware in the way one does become aware of such things that someone was watching her. She looked round at Modification Draughtsman, Biochemist, Quantity Surveyor. As she looked at the last she saw a head being bent rather too quickly over some papers—a young head, a young man. At that moment, as though he could not help himself, he looked up. Junia smiled. For a moment he hesitated, then he smiled back. The thaw at last, rejoiced Junia, smiling all the way now. The man smiled all the way, too, a little doubtfully at first, then brightly, sincerely. He returned to his work.

A few minutes later Renata came in. Junia had picked up a book on mineralogy from the desk and did not hear her until Renata said rather abruptly of the book: 'I hoped to read it if I found time. Time! What a laugh! I don't even find time to catch up with myself out here. I've just come from the hostel after an exhausting session with Joe, trying to get his next month's grocery order out of him. We have to have it for supplies. Didn't you see me crossing to the office?'

'I was reading,' said Junia.

'Yes.' Renata had taken the book from Junia, shut it, then put it away. 'I was waving to you as I came over,' she said. Somehow she seemed to make a point of it. Why, Junia did not know. She had not seen her, so she could have arrived from any direction. A thought occurred to Junia. Perhaps Renata had *not* been over at the hostel at all, perhaps she had been down at Colin's. Poor Renata, there was no need for her to conceal such a natural thing as a visit to Colin. Probably, being interested in Colin's book, she had got into the way of slipping down to ask the latest developments, the current chapter, and now she felt caught out … even guilty. She felt she should reassure Renata on this, then decided it might embarrass her. She let it pass and asked, instead, for something to do.

Renata produced some copying, dull routine stuff that Junia felt could have been put through the machine in the corner of the office while she tackled something more demanding. But again she let it pass, and worked silently until lunch.

It was not hunger that prompted her to look up at noon, for after all she had had a sound breakfast, and it was not Renata, it was the young quantity surveyor getting up from his desk in the adjoining office. He did it rather obviously, so Junia had to look up, and again, after a brief exchange of glances, they smiled at each other. The smile did not miss Renata, though she did not say anything then.

She did propose that they went across to the mess and ate, though, and when they got there Colin was already at the corner table. They decided on salads and had a pleasant meal together, free from Karl Kemble's rather uncomfortable fourth. Three, Junia found, in this instance was much more to her liking.

It was only towards the end of the meal that Renata mentioned the office.

'I see you've made friends with the quantity surveyor, Junia.'

'Oh, no, nothing like that, simply an exchange of looks.'

'Well, not to worry, he wouldn't be any use.'

'Use?' queried Junia.

'Peter wouldn't be.'

'Peter?'

'Peter Ferry, the Q.S. The quantity surveyor.'

'But—use?' Junia persisted.

'I mean you'd get nothing from him.' As Junia still looked nonplussed, Renata said quite sharply: 'I really meant that apart from a friendly soul among a host of unfriendlies, that would be all. Peter is young, new—but uninformed.'

'Uninformed?'

'Well, he couldn't——' Renata stopped, and a silence fell between them. Junia had a ridiculous feeling that though Colin was sitting and apparently not listening to a word, actually he was trying to convey something to Renata. Probably reproving her for dampening a friendly advance, Junia decided. She got up and crossed the room to renew her cup from the big pot.

When she returned to the table Renata gave her a rueful grin.

'Colin has just been bawling me out for criticising Peter. He says that Peter is a good stick, his only drawback that of being in the company of older men, and that you should encourage him.'

Colin said indignantly: 'I didn't put it that way, Renata—what sort of fiancé would I be if I told my girl to "encourage" someone? No, Junia dear, I just said to Renata that she was a little severe with Peter just now, and that I hoped you would take no notice of her. I would prefer you to be nice to the poor boy, he must get lonely. He's a new-chum, too, you see, only arrived here a few weeks before you did. You could join him at meals, perhaps, he eats by himself.'

'You mean we'll make a foursome? Renata, Mr Ferry, you, me?' It would be five of them when Karl Kemble came.

'Oh, no, Peter wouldn't join any party that included me,' said Colin firmly. 'He would have been indoctrinated already.'

'Indoctrinated?' said Junia, perplexed.

'Against the outsider.'

'I think you exaggerate, Colin.'

'Perhaps,' Colin said at once. 'But still be nice to him, Junia. He must feel out on a bough at his young age and in his position.'

'Of quantity surveyor?'

'The Q.S. Yes.'

'What exactly is a quantity surveyor?' asked Junia.

'What it sounds like,' inserted Renata knowledgeably, 'though nothing hush-hush as yet.'

'Hush-hush?' she asked.

'Oh, you greenhorn!' Renata smiled at her. 'All these projects are hush-hush, though not yet, I'd say, for young Peter. However, I could be wrong. I do know that Karl prefers a younger man and that quantity surveyors carry responsibility for all quantity take-offs.'

'All of which is beyond me,' dismissed Junia.

'It entails planning, estimating and cost controls, and though I don't think Peter——' There was another pause in the conversation, then Renata dropped the subject quite abruptly.

'You know, I think I'll follow Junia's example and have another cup. Will you, Colin?'

'Rule me out,' said Colin. 'I'm working on a new chapter this afternoon. If I consume too much I'll fall asleep. Goodbye, girls, see you at dinner.'

Renata got her second cup, and until they returned to the office the girls talked about Sydney as Junia last had seen it and as Renata hoped to see it on her leave.

'When are you being married, Renata?' Junia asked.

'I could ask the same of you,' smiled the lovely dark girl.

'When Colin's ready, I suppose,' admitted Junia wryly.

'Same answer for me, only substitute Karl for Colin.

Aren't men the world! Ready, Junia? Back to the salt mine.'

During the afternoon Junia thought of salt mines—no, not salt mines, salt farms, the salt farms that Karl had indicated from his Piper Cherokee. She remembered the rest of that wonderful flight. It had been pure magic, she thought.

'You have a dreamy expression,' Renata said. 'Don't tell me already there's more than a smile between you and our quantity surveyor.'

Junia laughed. 'I doubt if the smile will be repeated, let alone get any further than that.'

She was wrong. After Renata had made coffee in the afternoon she deliberately went across and tapped on Peter Ferry's window and held up a cup. For a very perceptible moment the young man hesitated, glanced around at the other glass windows, looked not at Renata but Junia, then stood up a little mutinously and crossed and opened the door.

'Would you?' Renata asked, still holding up the cup.

'Yes. Thank you.' The man said it to Renata, but he was looking at Junia. He smiled at her and Junia smiled back.

That was all there was to it, a cup of coffee and a small exchange of words. Peter did not waste any time after he had finished, he said 'Thank you' to Renata ... still looking at Junia ... and went back to his office.

'Mr Kemble hasn't been in all day,' Junia said later, to Renata.

'A little awkward when he's as far away as Melbourne.' Renata, who was filing, reached up to insert an envelope in a high drawer as she said it.

'Melbourne?' queried Junia.

'Yes.'

'But he never mentioned anything about that yesterday.' As soon as she had said it, Junia reddened. As though he would, or needed to, to her.

'Nor to me,' shrugged Renata. 'He must have flown down about some claim. That sort of thing is always done in a hurry.'

'A silent hurry?'

'Well, dear, you scarcely stand on a hill and shout out "Eureka, I've found it"!'

'I really meant wouldn't he tell you he was going, Renata?'

One of those infinitesimal pauses again, then Renata saying brightly: 'All these project bosses are the same, the land and what's in it comes first, and after that——' She shrugged a charming defeat.

'And you don't object?' admired Junia.

'Greater love hath no woman than to realise priorities. No, I don't mind. Anyway, how can I? It would still happen. I wonder what's in the wind this time, that wind that carries all our messages, is it more ore, more nickel or—gold?'

Junia gave a little shiver of excitement. 'It's thrilling, isn't it?'

'I'm glad you find it so because you just can't exist up here if you're not interested,' Renata said indulgently. 'Look, dear, why don't you cultivate young Ferry? I'm sure he would have lots of gen to tell you.'

'Wouldn't that be frowned on?' asked Junia.

'Not with Karl away, and he will be away for the rest of the week. The men take their cue from Karl, nobody else. At the very least you'd have a brief diversion.'

'Wouldn't the men think it odd me "cultivating" Peter, as you put it, when I'm engaged to Colin?'

'They wouldn't know you were engaged to Colin. Who would tell them, Junia? Colin doesn't speak to them, I barely speak to them and——'

'And Mr Kemble?'

'He would speak only about project stuff, nothing else. No, you could be interested and diverted, Junia. No time to get bored. Just for idle curiosity, anyway, pump our young Peter Ferry.'

'I don't want to pump anyone,' said Junia.

'I was only joking, silly, but all the same——'

Renata made a laugh of it, so Junia laughed, too, but, the day's work over, when Peter waited at the door to cross the road to the hostel with her, Junia did not hesitate to get into step beside him.

He was boyish and eager, a double attraction in this community of more matured, more deliberate men. He was very gratifying, she found, with his open admiration of her, very easy to talk to and—well, fun.

'I can't tell you how I felt when I first saw you sitting in the office,' he burst out. 'It was just like being transported back to civilisation.'

'You don't like it here?'

'Well, it's——'

'Different from what you thought?'

'Yes.'

They both laughed.

'I'm proud to be here, though,' Peter Ferry told Junia. 'It's quite a feather in my cap—I say, isn't that a crazy phrase, I never wear a cap.'

'I know what you mean, though. You mean Mr Kemble only employs the best.'

'Well . . .' He grinned and looked humble. 'The post was advertised widely, though,' he admitted proudly, 'and Mr Kemble was originally looking for a more matured experienced man.'

'But you had the qualifications?'

'Evidently. When he offered it to me, I rushed it. I mean, I never dreamed I'd snare a salary like I'm getting so early. But' ... ruefully ... 'I didn't dream, too, there'd be such—well, paucity of social life. I anticipated isolation, of course, but I saw a good community existence with it. Tennis after work, a pool.' A pause, then a frank shrug. 'Girls.'

'There was one.'

'Oh, yes, but——' He gave Junia an oblique look, oblique, anyway, for the pleasant, open boy he appeared to be, but he said no more. When it became apparent that he was not going to say anything, Junia insinuated helpfully:

'But the boss's property?'

'Yes,' he nodded gratefully. He did not seem anxious to talk about it, though, he seemed anxious to talk about the present ... and Junia.

'Then you happened,' he smiled. 'Eat with me tonight. That's awful, isn't it? I should be inviting you to an expensive French restaurant, not a project mess, and if I could I would, but none being available——'

'A beggar can't be a chooser? Yet Joe's food is very good.'

'But there's no candlelight.'

'No.' Junia had to giggle at that, the thought of candles on the scrubbed mess tables was just too much. Peter saw the funny side of it, too, and grinned.

'But will you?' he asked.

'Why not join us, Peter? Renata and Colin.' Junia waited for his reply.

'No ... no, I'm afraid not.'

'But why?'

'I don't think I can.' He looked away.

'But I've been eating all along with them, and——' They had reached the hostel now. 'Anyway, I must brush up. I'll see you later.' Junia smiled at him and went down the corridor to her room.

She decided to take a quick shower before dinner, and in the bathroom she heard the water splashing in the second of the recesses. It would have to be Renata.

'Hi there!' she called.

'Hi,' Renata returned. 'I waited for you, but Peter seemed to have taken over.'

'Yes, he's a nice boy.' Junia was now adjusting the spray. Over the flurry of drops she shouted: 'He's funny, too, he asked me very gallantly to dine with him. When we both realised where, we had to laugh.'

There was no more shower talk, but when Junia emerged cuddled in her towelling robe, Renata, in hers, was obviously waiting for her.

'Why not?' she said.

'Why not what?'

'Take pity on the poor boy and eat with him.'

'But he won't join our table,' said Junia. 'I asked him.'

'Then go to his table. I mean it, Junia. It must be beastly for him, a newcomer among all those established men.'

'He told me that he'd been flattered by the job but disappointed with the lack of social life.'

'Then cheer him up.'

'Colin——' Junia began.

'Would say the same. In fact he'd be the first to say it. He of all people knows what it is to be ignored.'

'Mr Kemble——'

'Isn't here,' reminded Renata, 'and anyway, I know that Karl' ... a pause ... 'that my Karl would be grateful to you.'

'Then why don't *you*——'

'Darling, I'm Karl's fiancée, remember.'

'And I'm Colin's.'

'But Colin, and I have to say it, Junia, is a much more

108

reasonable fiancé than Karl. He has tolerance, something I'm afraid my dear firebrand never has had.'

'Perhaps, but I still don't know, Renata,' sighed Junia uncertainly.

'You would be cheering him up no end. And you must know yourself how you felt when you first arrived here, a stranger, someone outside the group.'

'Yes,' agreed Junia, remembering that first night, her sinking feeling, her longing to escape somewhere else, her odd confusion at smelling jasmine instead of the tang of bush. Funny, she had still not solved that drift of jasmine. It must be some plant that the others had become familiar with, but that she, a newcomer, had recognised, or believed she recognised, as something else.

'Then?' Renata was urging.

'We'll see,' said Junia. 'I must hurry and dress now. I'll see you at dinner.'

'From Peter's table?'

But Junia would not promise that.

For the first time since her arrival here she found herself wishing she had something more feminine to put on. She eyed her shirts and trews with dissatisfaction, finding little consolation in the fact that they were clean, neat and not an impossible fit. She thought of her dresses in Sydney, and sighed . . . a sigh that had barely stopped when Renata opened the door and held up a shift.

'It won't be a perfect size for you since you're smaller, but as it's a loose garment it wouldn't matter. Try it on, anyway.'

'Oh, Renata, you think of everything!'

Renata smiled. 'It's just that I want skirts myself tonight, and I don't want to be the only one. There, it does fit you. It billows slightly, admittedly, but it's all the prettier for that, and the colour is certainly yours.'

Junia looked at the deep lush tones of the silk shift and could not agree, she felt that Renata's rich colouring was much more in keeping with the dramatic blues and tangerines, but since Renata was insistent, and since she felt like being a girl——

'Thank you,' she accepted.

'And you'll be nice to that nice boy?'

'I didn't say so.'

But the idea was fun. Someone new, like she was, someone not knowledgeable about Far-Off yet as Renata and Colin were, someone——

'I've spoken to Colin,' Renata was saying, 'he came up to return a book I'd loaned him. He thinks it's a good idea for both of you. He remembers what he went through.'

'Until you rescued him.'

'Oh, I didn't do that, I simply didn't exclude him like the rest.'

'Including Mr Kemble.'

'Karl has never been one way or another with Colin,' said Renata, 'he's just been——'

'Big Brother?'

'Well, I suppose that is the prerogative of a boss.'

'Perhaps, but he still doesn't talk to Colin.'

'My dear Junia, if you ever know Karl as I know him you'll know he doesn't talk to anyone. Not even me. I mean, not for talk's sake. And that piece of information comes from his nearest and dearest.' Renata bowed.

'Yes, be nice,' she said, and went out.

But Junia wasn't thinking of Peter now, she was thinking of three days out in the bush, of two nights, and of Karl Kemble *talking*. Talking to her from the tailboard of a truck. Talking from his sleeping bag across the wonderful, navy blue, plush desert night. Talking.

Yet, unlike Renata, I didn't know him, tumbled Junia's thoughts. I didn't know Karl Kemble at all.

CHAPTER EIGHT

PETER'S eyes lit up when Junia came into the mess in the borrowed dress. He was so prompt in coming forward, in insisting that she sat down while he brought her her tray, she had not the heart to tell him that she had finally decided that if they all did not eat together then she was sorry but Peter would have to eat alone. Before she quite realised it she was in a different corner from Renata's and Colin's, and the pair were smiling across at her, then deliberately finding something to occupy both their attentions so that they did not look across any more.

Amazingly ... amazing to Junia ... all the men present were the same. They glanced at the young pair, glanced quite tolerantly, then took no more notice.

'Don't tell me they're actually human,' Junia marvelled.

'The fellows?' queried Peter.

'Yes.'

'I'm sure they're a good bunch at heart. I haven't had the time to discover much yet.'

'My first impressions were bad,' she confided.

'Well, you know how it is in a place of this sort.'

'No, I don't.'

'It's co-operative,' he explained. 'No, not that exactly, but Mr Kemble has worked things out so that everyone has an active monetary interest as well as the interest of his work. It makes them—well——'

'Suspicious?' asked Junia with distaste.

'No, I really meant to imply more on their toes, on the watch, perceptive, looking after their own.'

'Naturally. Everyone does that.'

'I really meant,' Peter went on, reddening slightly, 'perhaps seeing possible trouble in someone—well, not in their own—their own——'

'Clique?'

'Well, I suppose that could be it, though it was not that word I was after.'

'But why are they more tolerant of me with you than me with Renata and Colin?' demanded Junia.

'Mr Brent is a foreigner here, isn't he?' pointed out Peter.

'Foreigner?'

'Not a company man. An outsider.'

'Well?'

'Well, projects are like that. I say, this isn't half bad, is it? Not dinner by candlelight but quite good.'

'But Renata is company.' Junia refused to be side-tracked. 'Also she's Mr Kemble's fiancée, so——'

'Yes,' nodded Peter. 'I see Joe has written up peaches and cream for sweets. Good show!'

Junia wondered what would happen if she told Peter that she herself was the 'foreigner's' fiancée, for obviously neither he, nor the men, as Renata had said, apparently knew. She wondered whether Peter would still see the meal out to the peaches and cream he was anticipating. About to be honest over it, she changed her mind. He was a nice boy and all this was harming nobody.

'Yes, peaches and cream will be great,' she smiled.

Over coffee, Peter said: 'Would you come out with me on your day off? I have a jalopy of sorts.'

'Where is there to go?' she asked.

'Some local spots I've found, and some I've been

told about. All worth seeing. I thought we could boil a billy.'

'That would be fun,' smiled Junia.

'Then you will?'

'Yes. But I don't know when my day off will be. After all, I've only just started.'

'Find out, and I'll fit mine with yours. I'll take you out to the Gap. Don't ask me why it's the Gap, I couldn't see anything like a gap. But there are wild-flowers you'll like.'

'Thank you. That will be nice.'

'Thank you for being nice.'

When Junia related the conversation later to Renata and Colin, Renata said that Junia must certainly take a day off and go ... go soon.

'But the quantity surveyor said he would fit his stand-down with mine. There's no hurry.'

Renata glanced at Colin and Colin cleared his throat and said: 'I think you should waste no time, dear. I have a feeling I'll be winding up my book earlier than I thought, and I would like you to leave Far-Off with a little more knowledge of the countryside than one bare street.'

'But I have much more knowledge, Colin. Mr Kemble took me up in his plane, remember. Also there was the getting to here——'

'Yes, but it's still a small canvas, Junia. Go, dear, while you have the chance.'

'Then you wouldn't mind?'

'Of course not.'

'And you, Renata?' she asked.

'Why should I mind?'

'My work——'

'Oh, that. I'll work you double hard when you get back. No, go, Junia. And Junia, take a memo and pencil

114

and make notes. I'm sure our Q.S. will be glad to tell *you* anything you ask, and knowledge is always handy. I mean, of course, it would help Colin's book.'

'Yes,' agreed Junia, quite looking forward to the exploration. She paused. 'When?'

'Why not this week?'

'This week?'

'Yes. We're not busy. And that's one of the things you learn up here, never to postpone anything if it's at all possible, in case the chance doesn't come again.'

'But I'd feel guilty relaxing so soon, especially——'

'Especially?'

'Well—with Mr Kemble away.'

'My dear, even if he were here, it would be the same. You could scarcely say he was a—well, hovering boss.'

'I haven't had him yet for a boss.'

'No, but he's still not——'

'Hovering?'

'Watching you. Oh, I know' ... a laugh from Renata ... 'that Colin calls him Big Brother, but I don't think he's been that to you.'

'No, he hasn't been that,' Junia said a little unevenly. Often, since they had come to Far-Off, she had thought she might as well be a piece of furniture ... and yet what else could she expect? She was nothing to him, only something that had been thrust on him and he had been kind enough, no, *resigned* enough, to accept.

'Then have fun, Junia,' repeated Renata, 'for Colin has just told you that quite soon you two might flit off.'

'Yes, he has.' Junia knew she should feel glad about that, but—well, she wasn't. She did not look at Colin. She did not want him to see the disappointment in her face, be disappointed himself, or she did not *want* to leave Far-Off. Not yet, anyway. Indeed, the way she felt at this juncture, eager, curious, waiting for more, *not at all*.

Renata, watching her with slight puzzlement, said: 'Yes, go. See the place.'

'Very well, you two persuaders, I think I will.'

When Junia told Peter that she would definitely accept his invitation, the young quantity surveyor's face lit up eagerly.

'Wonderful! I'm off duty tomorrow. We work our own hours here, choose our own time for relaxation, and I feel like tomorrow.' He grinned at her.

'You forget I'm a worker, too,' Junia warned, 'but haven't yet accumulated any days as it seems you have.'

'No, but you can still make up for them afterwards.'

'When I've barely begun?'

'I'm sure Mr Kemble——' Peter began.

'Then I'm not sure. Anyway, he's away, remember.'

'Yes.' Peter looked so deflated that Junia said at once:

'But Renata is my superior and I've already asked her and she's said Yes.' She hadn't really, Renata had suggested it all herself, but it seemed hardly the right thing to tell Peter how the subject had already been aired and debated. Anyway, Peter's radiant face at her announcement made the evasion worthwhile.

Peter had spoken first about the Gap, and it was to the Gap first that they went. Karl Kemble had brought him out here soon after he had arrived at Far-Off, Peter related, partly to give him an idea of where he was and partly to introduce him to the Pinji tribe, who were their nearest neighbours, even to the extent of one of the men being in Kemble's employ.

'Yes, I have met Jimmy,' nodded Junia.

'Jimmy is the boss's right hand, he never goes bush without him. Jimmy is very proud of the trust the boss puts in him. As we pass the camp you'll see the Far-Off truck there. Mr Kemble allows Jimmy to bring it out.'

'Aren't we calling in?' asked Junia with disappointment of Peter's 'As we pass the camp.'

Peter shook an emphatic head. 'Lesson Number One, Mr Kemble told me, is you don't call in, you get invited, also the invitation must come from the Number One, or Top, man. This is a very old tribe, practically only emerged to present-day living in the last few years, and Mr Kemble says that these things count.'

'Well,' said Junia with satisfaction, 'at least I can wave, and I don't think that wave back just now came from the Number One man.'

'From Jimmy?'

'Yes.' They were almost past the camp now, and Junia was giving a last salute to Jimmy, who had been bent over the engine of the lorry before he had straightened at the sound of their car. She had smiled as Jimmy obviously recalled her, smiled at his frantic waving.

'You were on the track with Mr Kemble, weren't you?' asked Peter.

'And Jimmy, yes.'

'Lucky Boss. Lucky Jimmy.'

'I don't know about Jimmy, but I do know that Mr Kemble considered himself very unlucky,' Junia laughed.

She was glad that at that moment they reached the Gap so that Peter did not pursue the subject. The lorry in which she had hidden herself for four uncomfortable hours, its driving cabin she had shared, its tailboard she had also shared, had started a flood of memories.

'Well,' she commented, looking around, 'there's no gap, as you said, but it's certainly pretty.'

It was. Even without the recent big rains that had

altered it from bare land to a place of flowers it still would have caught the attention. There were rocks flung artlessly about as though a family of giants had been playing a game of Catch with them, then suddenly wearied. They were irregular stones, not only in size and shape but in colour. There were pottery golds, old ochres, blood reds and dramatic purples.

For the rest, there was the usual sparse shade, since what trees grew here, grew stunted. Since they were naturally small trees, small through many centuries of drought, the Wet had been unable to do anything with them as it had with everything else, but the flood flowers had. Some of the mulgas were wreathed from bottom to top bough with yellow daisy.

Peter was gathering sticks to make a fire. Junia helped him, and soon they were enjoying his promised billy tea.

'I think that rightly I should circle the billy twice to draw the brew,' Peter submitted, 'but I'm not up to that yet. I'll have to ask Mr Kemble.'

But Karl Kemble did not intrude in the pleasant hour that followed. Peter drew Junia out about her life before she had come here and she told him as much as she thought he should know. In return he told her a little about himself. There was not much, he shrugged, to tell, in fact as little as any man could have. He left it at that, and with acceptance on both sides they talked idly on other subjects, ate, drank, then dozed in the hot gold sun. The time flew.

Renata was a little critical later when Junia came back to Far-Off with an unopened notebook.

'I thought you wanted to learn something of the place,' she said.

'But I did learn. I never knew a rock could run such a gamut of colours.'

'I meant ... Oh, it doesn't matter, dear. So nice to know you enjoyed yourself. Where will you go next?'

'Do you think I should?'

'Oh, Junia, not that again?'

'Well, Peter did mention a wurlie ... you know about wurlies?'

'Old watering holes, yes.'

'Peter saw this one on an exploratory trip with Mr Kemble. It was the last one before Mr Kemble went south.'

'I see,' said Renata. 'Now we're getting somewhere.'

'What do you mean, Renata?'

'I mean when you see this wurlie it will be something quite different, won't it?' Renata smiled at Junia. 'Do take notes this time. For your own ... and Colin's ... benefit.'

'... Colin's? Oh, the book.'

'Yes, the book.'

The afternoon at the wurlie proved quite as enjoyable as the Gap. Junia was delighted with the green water caught up in a circle of rocks and shaded by overhanging bark trees until it became as dark and mysterious as any mountain pool, in spite of its location.

Peter related what Karl Kemble had related to him, how once it had been an aboriginal watering-hole, in fact it had been the life source of the Pinjis, Jimmy's tribe, when they had lived further out. They had found a nearer source, and now the hole had been taken over by the bush and the bush beings. You could even see the pad marks on the earth below the rocks cradling the wurlie.

If they had had a hide, Peter regretted, they could have watched the bush beings, watched the wallabies, lizards, grass rats and snakes coming for water. Wild

119

dogs, too, for there were distinct dingo marks on the sand surrounds.

They proved the existence of dingoes soon after in the discovery of a small yellow pup. He had white flashes on his paws and his ears were pricked and elfin. They took him along to the Pinjis from which he had probably strayed, and even if he hadn't belonged once would still be welcome, for there was a close affinity between the aboriginal and the wild dog.

'Not so wild, I'd say,' Peter laughed, 'once he's in the camp. Probably then he's as domesticated as any Fido.'

If Renata was disappointed with Junia's notebook that night, she never said so. Instead she listened quietly to Junia's account of how Peter had first approached the wurlie.

'He told me the party was looking for signs,' Junia said. She asked: 'Is that right, Renata? Signs?'

'Quite right, dear. We'll make a geologist of you yet. But signs out there!'

'I don't think any were found, only the wurlie ... oh, and an old prospector with a dolly pot.'

'What?' queried Renata.

'A prospector. Peter was recounting it to me ... the hat with the bobbing corks for flies and the tucker bag.'

'Yes?'

'That's all,' said Junia. 'He never did any talking with him, only Mr Kemble did.'

'Interesting. And all this was near the wurlie?'

'On the way there.'

'You took the track by the Pinji camp, didn't you?'

'Peter always does, Renata. It's a good landmark, he says. Oh, dear, I'm sorry I never got anything for Colin.'

'Not to worry,' Renata assured her, 'so long as you had a good day.'

They had more explorations, and Peter mentioned

during one of them a possible visit to the coast.

'I've already been to the coast with Mr Kemble,' Junia said.

'Yes, you flew, but what you see on top is not what you see below. It's magnificent, of course, but not——'

'Intimate?'

'Exactly, Junia.'

'Wouldn't it be too far by surface?' asked Junia.

'That's what I'm coming to. There are hotels in the coastal boom towns ... well, one hotel a town, anyway ... and we could make several days of it. One for getting there, maybe one for being there, one for getting back. I really do intend to go myself, in fact, Junia, it's one of my dearest wishes, so if you'd like to come——'

'Oh, I would, but——'

'But?'

'But I think a trip of that proportion should wait until Mr Kemble's return.' Junia really mean '... should wait for Mr Kemble's permission.' But she would not say so.

'Perhaps,' Peter nodded. 'But keep it in mind, won't you?'

As it turned out it was another week before the boss flew back to Far-Off, and in that time the two young people fitted in as many trips as they could, on the days when they did not go adventuring working longer hours at the office to make up for their sojourns, Peter at his desk, Junia at the typewriter, occasionally looking up and smiling at each other, the rest of the men appearing quite tolerant of it all. As for Renata, she helped Junia in every way, so that Junia never had any reason to say No to any new invitation from Peter. Colin, too, whom Junia had asked quite frankly about it all, whether he really was minding, or not, was most agreeable, telling Junia again that she might as well see as much as she could before time ran out. Before time ran out. Junia found herself withdrawing ... actually withdrawing ... from that.

By the Wednesday when the Cherokee flew in from the country airfield at which Kemble had left it while he took a larger passenger plane south, Junia felt she had a good idea of the terrain around her.

When she heard the Cherokee, she took no notice; small planes often went over, and, from the sour looks on the men's faces, for no good reason, but evidently they recognised this beat as the home beat, and she saw them nod to each other and heard them call: 'Boss's back!'

Renata went out to bring him in, but Junia did not see him arrive, and, since she had finished her day's work and returned to the hostel, she did not see him go straight to his office, and there have a word with each of his officers in turn.

When at last she did see him it was in the mess, and she and Peter were eating together once more in their particular corner table. Dinner by candlelight, as Peter had put it wryly in the beginning, had become quite an established thing with them by now.

Karl Kemble nodded coolly to Junia, but, as far as Junia could tell, he did not speak to Peter.

However Peter, watching Junia, said at once: 'No, it's all right, I've been talking with K.K. this afternoon, and' ... a smile ... 'he's not at all put out about us.'

'About us?' she questioned.

'Well, my showing you around ... hands across the table, all that.'

'Oh, Peter, we don't!' Junia protested.

'Hands across the table? No, not yet, but it's what I'm leading up to,' Peter laughed.

'You're impossible!'

'I hope not, Junia. I'm trusting not. Not impossible. Not for you.' He smiled again at Junia, and it was hard not to smile back at his fresh, nice face.

Junia was a little let down when Karl Kemble carried his tray to Renata's and Colin's table. Although he always remained civil with Colin, it was very obvious he had no time for him. Still, she thought, Renata being his fiancée it was only to be expected that he ate there. Yet she was Colin's fiancée and eating here. Oh, it was all too ridiculous. She started to laugh.

'I didn't want you to find it funny,' Peter reproached, still on his own theme of what he wanted from life.

Junia laughed again.

Towards the end of the meal, the big boss joined them.

'I hate breaking up dinner by candlelight ... oh, yes, Renata told me all about that ... but I thought I'd inflict myself on you for coffee. You do the honours, Peter, you play mother.'

'Mother!' said Peter in disgust.

'Ah, so that's how it is,' Karl said as Peter moved away to manipulate three cups. 'Peter would sooner another role? Yet what about your fiancée, Miss West?'

'Colin is agreeable ... I really mean he wants me to— well——' Junia paused. Something urged her not to say more about that, not to tell Karl Kemble that, as they were leaving quite soon, Colin believed she should see as much as she could of this place, that she should go around with Peter.

'Yes? He wants you to——?'

'To enjoy myself.'

'A very remarkable fiancé,' said Karl dryly.

There was silence for a few moments.

'Do *you* mind, Mr Kemble?' Junia ventured.

'I?'

'Yes. Do you mind?'

'If Mr Brent doesn't, why should I?'

'I meant mind because I've been out quite a lot—from the office, that is. But I assure you I haven't neglected my work. I even worked extra hours ... and so did Peter.'

'Of course.'

Peter was still busy with the coffee, he was not at all practised in it.

'You'll have to teach him, won't you?' Karl Kemble smiled lazily as he watched the young man.

'Why should I? I mean, it's nothing to do with me.'

'No? Then I think perhaps you should let *him* know that. I've been among men all my life, Miss West, and that look on his face when I came up just now was scarcely that.'

'Scarcely what?' asked Junia.

'Scarcely nothing-to-do-with-me.'

'What do you mean?'

'I think you know.'

There was a silence for a few moments, a sullen variety of silence.

'I think you do mind,' Junia burst out. 'I think you feel I haven't been giving you your money's worth.' It was not what she wanted to say, but she could hardly tell him to keep his opinions on Peter to himself.

'Money's worth?' Kemble asked idly.

'For the work I'm expected to do for you.'

'I don't believe there's been any money exchange as yet, has there? However, perish that thought. Believe me, I would always collect my pounds of flesh.'

'Yes, I believe you would,' said Junia dryly.

A few moments went by.

'Well, if your fiancé doesn't object to you going out with someone else, eating with someone else, why should it concern me?' Karl Kemble said almost with boredom.

'Exactly,' Junia agreed.

'... Unless' ... slyly ... '*I* became involved.' Karl Kemble was looking at Junia keenly now, Junia knew that even though she kept her own eyes down.

'Involved?' she asked, still not looking up.

'Yes, I said involved.'

'How do you mean?'

'There could be several answers to that,' he suggested smoothly. 'Think it over.'

'I still wouldn't know what you meant.'

'Then I'll give you the more obvious answer ... just for a laugh.' He laughed himself. 'Unless I became involved in this small happening by taking over Peter's role from him.'

'Peter has had no role, not with me, he's merely driven me around.'

'That's among the things I meant. Oh, I know I've flipped you to the coast, but there's still many things to show you that I believe your Peter hasn't done yet.'

'Like?'

'Like a western morning star, Junia West? Like the one you disbelieved when I told you about it? Has Peter shown you that yet?'

'No, but——'

'Then we must fix that, mustn't we? Tomorrow morning at three. It has to be three to give us time to drive out there.'

'Out where?' she asked.

'You'll see. I'll throw pebbles on your window ... oh, yes, I know which window ... and if you don't come I'll——'

'Mr Kemble, I——' About to refuse, refuse angrily, Junia became aware of something hard and indomitable and unsmiling in his now narrowed eyes, something she could not turn away from, could not fight. Could not disobey.

'Yes, Miss West?'

'No need for the pebbles. I'll be there,' she said meekly instead.

'Then just as well, for there are no pebbles around here, only rocks,' he laughed lightly.

'Bad for windows.' Junia heard herself saying it and wondered that she could do it so blandly, almost as blandly as he did. It must be catching, she thought; bland dislike must be something you contacted from this bland disliking man.

She looked over at Peter struggling across with a tray of coffee. Poor Peter!

'Well, of all the——' Peter started to say, and looking back to the table again, Junia could not blame him.

Karl Kemble had left.

CHAPTER NINE

AROUND two in the morning Junia woke automatically as though an inner alarm had been set. Or pebbles thrown against a window? She checked the time, then decided to get up at once since she feared she might drift off again, and that man, that Karl Kemble, would be as good as his word—and his warning. Perhaps he would not throw rocks, but she would not put it past him actually to come in here and shake her awake.

Well, Mr Kemble, Junia thought grimly, I'm going to surprise you, I'm going to be waiting for you. Since she had plenty of time, and since a shower would make her more alert, a condition she very much desired just to show that boss, she decided to do just that: to shower. The bathroom was isolated, so she should disturb no one. Anyway, she thought, now tiptoeing down the passage, at this end there was only Renata to disturb, and if she went very quietly ...

She stopped her pussyfooting, plainly puzzled, or at least puzzled at first. Renata's light was on. She could see the beam under the door.

She went instinctively forward to tap on the door, ask if everything was all right. Then she paused. Renata might be having a sleepless night, even younger people did upon occasion, and might resent such an intrusion. Or she might have felt like a cup of coffee, or had an urge to read a book, or—— Anyway, what sort of fool would she, Junia, look after she had tapped and inquired and after Renata had asked why she, Junia, was up herself? How could you answer to a fiancée that you were going with *her* fiancé to see a morning star?

Fiancé. Fiancée. Weren't those two rather an odd couple? Still, couldn't the same be said lately about Colin and herself?

No, Junia decided not to tap, so she crept on. As she turned the corner that led to the second passage she saw Renata's beam go black again, and felt glad she had not interfered ... but as she reached the bathroom and opened the door she distinctly heard the sound of steps. Descending steps. The steps down Karl Kemble's 'handy' ... 'convenient' exit sprang at once to Junia's mind. Now why, she wondered, had he ever said that?

In spite of herself and her good sense, Junia was frowning as she turned on the hot tap, but when she finished bracingly with a turn of the cold tap, she had forgotten the episode, and was only thinking curiously about that curious man she was soon to meet, that man who insisted on showing her a morning star.

She tiptoed back ... darkness now in Renata's room ... and dressed. Congratulating herself, she reached the main entrance fifteen minutes early. That would show him.

'Good morning.'

Karl Kemble leaned across to the passenger's door of his parked wagon and opened it. He did not get out to help her, and as Junia, fuming inwardly at his calm acceptance of her early arrival, climbed in she noticed his only half-concealed smile of triumph. He had anticipated that she would come early, so he had beaten her to it.

He said nothing, though, as he turned the wagon out of Far-Off's one road and hit ... well, Junia could not have said where they hit, whether it was north, south, east or west, it was far too dark to see.

She must have muttered something of the sort, for he turned in his driving seat and said in assumed surprise: 'But of course it's dark, it has to be dark. We've come to trap the morning star, not the evening.'

'I don't know why.'

'You do, though. To prove that the star is not bedraggled as once you said it was but all the brightness of Heaven.'

'You're being ridiculous,' she smiled.

'But poetic?'

'Still ridiculous.'

'Perhaps,' he conceded with a shrug. 'Then shall we say instead all the ingredients of Paradise?'

'Paradise lost?'

There was an abrupt jerk as the man stopped the wagon without any warning. He turned in his seat to Junia.

'Paradise not yet found,' he corrected her abruptly.

'Mr Kemble,' Junia said stiffly, 'I don't understand you.'

'Do you want to?'

She did not answer.

'Do you want to—Junia?'

Now he was silent as well as he waited for her answer. In the quiet Junia could hear all the things one hears in bush silences, the stirrings, the whirrings, the little sighs and movements.

'I—I don't know what you're talking about,' she said at last, and she spoke abruptly. 'Please, if we don't go now we shall miss the star.'

'And all the brightness of Heaven?'

'Or of Paradise either lost or not yet found,' Junia shrugged.

'Practical Miss West! An alternative for everything.' He found gears and they moved forward again, this time without any exchange of words, which he must have needed, for Junia never could have picked a way herself in the dark obscurity, and she marvelled that Karl Kemble did.

'Familiarity.' Evidently he read her wonder, so answered it.

'Then you drive girls regularly to see morning stars?' she said flippantly to hide something she could not have explained, even to herself.

Again, even more abruptly than before, the wagon stopped.

'Never before,' Karl Kemble said. 'Never again.' He began moving once more.

This time the silence was absolute until he reached wherever he had intended to reach, and it seemed to Junia like a slight hill. Then, still not speaking, he braked.

Still in silence they waited. It was only a few breaths from piccaninny daylight now, Junia judged, and she held her own breath, though there was nothing to see yet. There was also nothing to hear. In a bush quiet there was always something unquiet, a stir, a slither, a turning, a sigh. But now there seemed nothing at all. The sky was still obscure, except that it seemed a slightly paler obscurity. But there was to be no wand waving of dark night into bright morning, Junia decided, no sudden blaze, no——

And then it happened. Not the bedraggled little city star she had argued about with the man beside her, argued out in the bush, yet not the blaze that his stubborn insistence had seemed to suggest, but more—well, more a blossoming of a star. First a faint prick, then a shy light, then the little star emerging like a shining flower. Yes, a flowering, a blossoming. A blossoming, too, the sudden feel of his hand seeking in the dark, then entrapping hers, her own hand instinctively holding his in return, then two people turning to each other in the fading dark and marking a moment in a kiss, a gentle kiss at first, but fast gaining depth and feeling, gaining them as quickly as the little star had blossomed, that single kiss filling each of them, just as the star now seemed to be filling the morning sky. A single kiss filling their world.

They clung to each other, and it was only when a scudding cloud obliterated the star for a moment that they drew apart.

What happened? Junia was thinking. She did not look at Karl.

He did not speak for several minutes, in fact not until the star had escaped the cloud and again sailed the now fast-lightening sky. Then: 'So!' he said to her in indication, and spread his big hands, the hands that had now released her. Then he asked: 'Shall we go home again?'

He started the car. It was not so hazardous now, the bush, though still dark, found shapes to warn the driver. Junia had no need to be nervous any more, and anyway, even if it had still been dark she knew she would not have thought about it. The events of the last few minutes had pushed everything else aside.

If it had just been one of them, then she knew she could put it all out of her mind, or at least have *tried*. But the response just now had been from the two of them. Of that she was sure.

They drove along in complete silence. A quick look at the man beside her intent on threading a way between the mulga and bark trees convinced Junia that Karl had no intention of breaking the silence, must be any break in the imposed quiet, imp_ made by her.

She wanted no breaking of it, yet there was something she knew she had to ask. Surely he wanted to ask it back of her.

She wet her lips but could find no words. He must have sensed the questioning in her, for he asked, and his voice was uncompromisingly harsh for some reason:

'Yes?'

'Nothing,' she said hastily.

'What was it you wanted to say to me?'

'Nothing—I told you. I mean——'

'Well?'

'Renata.' Junia said the girl's name with a gulp.

'What about Renata?'

'She is—your fiancée,' she faltered.

'Well?'

'But just now——'

'Yes?'

'Just now——' she began again.

'Just now I kissed you? You kissed me back? Is that what you're trying to mumble?'

'Yes.' Wretchedly.

'Then what about it?'

'Doesn't she . . . I mean wouldn't she—mind?'

'Isn't that for you to find out?'

'I could say the same to you,' Junia reminded him.

'But it would be unnecessary,' he assured her blandly, 'I know.'

'If you're speaking of——'

'I'm speaking, of course, of Colin Brent—of the man you love. And now, Miss West, please to stop these introspections. We're coming to the town, so sit up and be . . .

'Ermal.'

call that b. out of the bush at this early hour! You

'Morning stars occur only at early hours, so it would have to be normal.'

They had reached the hostel by now. Karl leaned across Junia and began opening the door for her. 'A shower will bring you down to earth,' he suggested laconically.

'I was on earth before, and anyway, I've had one—a shower, I mean.' She thought of that beam that had shone from Renata's door and added more to herself: 'Poor Renata mustn't have slept well, her light was on when I went to the bathroom.'

She said it abstractedly, but his interest in return was anything but abstracted. About to push open the door, he halted.

'Did you pause to speak to them?' he asked deliberately.

'Them? What on earth are you talking about? Renata's light was on, she had no one else there. Probably was reading, or making coffee. Anyway, when I came back again the light was out.' Junia stopped. She was thinking, and with curiosity now, about that sound of steps down the 'handy . . . convenient' stairway.

Karl was looking at her narrowly. 'Is that all?'

'Is what all?'

'What you've just told me.'

'Of course it is. What else? How absurd you are!'

'Yes. Absurd.' He opened the door and nodded for her to get out. 'No need to tell Renata about the morning star,' he shrugged, 'she's seen many.'

'I expect so.'

'Both evening and midnight, too.'

'Of course.' Junia got out and ran up the steps and went into the hostel without looking back. 'Renata has seen many' rang in her ears. No need to ask with whom she had seen them. Had it been on a small far hill, and

133

had Renata turned and had he turned and—— Junia turned herself into the corridor. The long building was still inactive, the hall empty. Renata's door closed.

Junia went into her own room, and, glancing at her watch, decided to avail herself of an hour's rest before she officially got up. After all, *he* would be in attendance today, so he must find her as he would undoubtedly always be, and that was fighting fit.

Fighting fit? Passing the mirror as she crossed to her bed, she saw her reflection, and had to smile. A rueful smile, for what other sort of smile could there be at that now wan countenance? The bedraggled star. That was what she had called the morning star before she had seen it out here, but now she said bedraggled instead to herself. For a few moments out there in the bush she had felt—had felt as she had never felt before, not in all her life. She had not known why, nor wanted to examine it, she had just felt——

But now she was really a morning star, her city version, not his. Not any brightness of Heaven, nor Paradise either. Not anything at all. Just Junia.

With a resigned shrug she lay down.

Junia must have dozed, or drifted, or something, because when she opened her eyes again she was horrified when she looked at the clock. Not only had she missed breakfast, which didn't matter, anyway, but already she was late for work. She was annoyed with herself for slipping off. Of all days this was the day she wanted to appear fresh and punctual. Now, even if she skipped a cup of coffee, a freshening splash, she would be half an hour late. He, he who would never be late, would note her tardiness, and raise his brows.

She fumbled her feet into her shoes and splashed her face regardless. Otherwise she might not have been sufficiently awake to leave the hostel and cross the road to the office. With luck, she thought, as she did so, he might not be there, he might have been called out. He even ... extravagant thought ... might not have turned up himself. He might have lain down, too, as she had, and lost consciousness.

But no such luck. She saw that the moment she entered. Karl Kemble was in his glassed office, and he was either dictating or discussing something with Renata. In aggravation Junia sat down at her desk, but not before Peter caught her eye from his quantity surveyor's glass cage and smiled a good morning. Relieved that at least she was welcome there, Junia smiled back.

She looked around for something to do; she felt a fool just sitting there. She tried to keep her glance directly before her, not slant it to Peter, which would be noticed and disapproved of by Big Brother, and certainly not to Big Brother himself to be silently chastened for arriving late.

But inevitably, and she should have known it, Junia did look towards Karl Kemble's office. Renata was bent over some papers and did not see her glance, but Karl did. He looked blankly back at Junia, then, deliberately Junia felt, obviously meaning Junia to see, he laid his arm on Renata's. Putting everything into its right place, its right perspective, Junia interpreted it. She felt it was his way of telling her she had been a fool when she had questioned him on their way back from waiting for a star. She felt shamed and rather ridiculous, and she scrabbled blindly again for something to do, anything to do, but all she unearthed was a small memo of figures that she could not follow pushed well under Renata's papers. Little use to type these, she thought, when she did not understand what they were about. However, it seemed something to make her look occupied, so she inserted a sheet of paper in the machine and began automatically transcribing. She finished the list and took out the sheet just as Renata left the boss's office. Before she could offer them to Renata with the excuse that she had had to do something, Renata said brightly:

'Coffee, Junia? I'm sure you must need some. Karl has just told me you didn't turn up for breakfast.'

'No.' Junia wondered if Karl, too, had told Renata why, had described the early morning pilgrimage. He had said that she had no need to ... 'Renata has seen many stars' ... but there would be a different rule for him.

'As you know, I never have breakfast,' went on Renata, plugging in, 'so don't feel awful about it, dear.'

'But I was late,' said Junia.

'I told you before we choose our own hours here. I just happen to be an early starter,' Renata smiled.

'And I haven't even started.' Junia had, but she felt absurd now, proffering a paper to Renata that had not been called for. Surreptitiously she pushed it under a book on her desk.

'We'll keep you back tonight,' teased Renata. She seemed in a very good mood. 'I'll even run down and tell Colin the bad news, but then, of course, you'll see him yourself at lunch.'

She made coffee, found work for Junia, and the morning pushed on.

Junia did see Colin at lunch, but she also saw the rest of them, for in some unexplained way, and obviously not to Peter's liking, they all shared the same table today. Gone the cosy tête-à-têtes, Peter's disappointed look said, probably gone, too, the evening's pretend meals by candlelight.

Karl Kemble was in a talkative mood. He even included Colin in his conversation.

'I took our Miss West out to see what morning stars look like out west,' he announced clearly to the entire table. A pause. '*Anyone* mind?'

No one answered.

Now Karl Kemble laughed heartily.

'I'm not asking this on my own initiative,' he continued, 'I'm asking for our Miss West.' He bowed ironically to Junia. 'She was a little uneasy about it, you see. Wanted reassurance from—Renata.' Now his amused eyes were turned to his fiancée. 'I advised her to ask you herself. Did she?'

No one answered, but everyone smiled—including Junia. If she hadn't smiled, she would have stood out, she thought. She did not know about the other smiles, she couldn't know, but her own smile was frozen. What sort of man was this?

The topic changed, fortunately, but Peter, who had become silent, did not join in with the easier conversation. When Junia rose to bring back more coffee, he got up, too, to help her carry it.

'You might have told me you wanted to go,' he reproached her as she poured and creamed.

'To see the star?'

'Yes.'

'Oh, it was nothing,' she shrugged.

'Perhaps so, but I've come to think of us as doing things together lately, Junia.'

'But you must have known you shouldn't,' Junia said quickly, forgetting that Peter knew nothing about Colin, and still wouldn't know. Mr Kemble had addressed no one in particular just now, he had said: '*Anyone* mind?' and left it at that.

She bit her lip ... then drew a determined breath. She felt it was time that Peter was told.

'Peter——' she began.

But Peter was bearing back the tray of coffee and looking not quite so deflated as before. That 'Oh, it was nothing' must have brightened him slightly.

The meal finished, but today for some reason Karl, who was always a fast eater, seemed unusually slow. The others had risen before he finished his coffee, and he waved them on ... but at the same time he detained Junia.

'I have some work to catch up,' Junia tried, 'I was late this morning.'

'I noticed. And you'll catch up, don't worry. But I want a word with you.'

'As a matter of fact,' Junia observed coldly, 'I want one with you.'

They were quite alone now. He sat back and invited: 'Say your word first.'

'Was it necessary to speak like you did just now?'

'What did I say? Let me think. Oh, yes, that the roast beef was good.'

'About my not asking Renata,' she persisted.

'Well, you didn't, did you?'

'But did you have to mark it important by making such a topic of it?'

'Did I?' he shrugged. 'I didn't notice. And I don't believe anyone else took much notice, either, unless it was our quantity surveyor. His lip did drop.' He grinned.

'It was all in bad taste,' said Junia.

'I merely said something you wanted to say but couldn't find the nerve.' He paused. 'And yet——'

'Yes?'

'And yet you have the nerve to rummage round with things that don't belong to you.'

'I beg your pardon?' she queried.

'It will have to be more than that, Miss West, more

than asking of pardons. You'd better get on your knees and cry for a reprieve.'

'A reprieve? What on earth are you talking about?'

'Figures. Figures recorded neatly and concealed carefully for the moment under a book, a book you had the misfortune for me to need almost as soon as you had typed and hidden them.' He looked at her narrowly. 'What's the game, Miss West?'

'Game?' she echoed.

'That's what I said.'

'I still don't understand you.'

'Then understand this.' He reached in his pocket and took out the sheet she had copied from Renata's small memo so as to have something ... anything ... to occupy herself. He placed it directly in front of her.

'I still don't understand,' Junia persisted. 'I don't understand you.'

'But you intended handing this to someone who does understand?'

'No, of course not. Why should I?'

'You tell me, young lady, then I'll tell you.'

'I—I felt a fool not having anything to do this morning, so—so I typed what I did.'

'Just like that?'

'Just like that.'

'I see. And from where did you get the gen?'

'Gen?' she queried, perplexed.

'From where did you copy this?'

She hated him now, she hated his suspicion, his thinned lips, his narrowed eyes, his air of ruthless waiting.

'I don't know. I think it was just around.'

'Around where?' he demanded.

'Around, about—oh, I don't know. On the desk, on the floor. Given to me.'

'By whom?'

'I don't know, I tell you!' she said crossly. 'I can't remember.'

'By our young Q.S.?'

'Certainly not!'

'Yet you do see a lot of him,' he pointed out.

'I have also ... today ... seen a lot, too much, of you.' Junia rose.

Karl rose with her. The dining room had emptied. Joe was in his kitchen and the invisible man again.

'You'll be seeing more,' Karl warned.

'I don't believe so,' she said triumphantly. 'I believe Colin is almost ready to leave.'

'In which case you'll certainly be seeing a lot more of me.'

'What do you mean?'

'What I said.'

'You're a very strange man,' Junia said in a tight voice. She could not understand him ... and she wanted to. She did not know why she wanted to, but she did, and that made for the almost unbearable tightness in her.

He made a step forward, but before he could speak again she had slipped away.

She crossed to the office and was working by the time he entered. He did not look her way, his attention was on a book he had on his desk. It was the book under which she had slipped the typed copy. He must have found he needed the book, removed it, then discovered what she had done.

Well, there could be no harm in it, otherwise Renata would not have had the information in a small memo for anyone to take up—still, she had had to turn things over to find it, Junia recalled troublously, 'scrabbled' had been her word. She had had to *look*.

140

Renata smiled across the desk at her at that moment, and Junia smiled back. At least Renata did not know the storm in a teacup, for that was all it must be, she felt. She heard the master door open and shut. Karl Kemble went out.

'So,' cheered Renata, 'you needn't make up that time after all, Junia. Not with Big Brother gone.'

Junia forced a grin back at Renata. 'I will, though. I'd feel guilty.'

'Never feel guilty,' Renata advised. 'But if you're persistent about doing a day's work, I'll let Colin know, because I don't believe you told him at lunch.'

'No one else,' Junia reminded her wryly, 'told anything at lunch.'

When the others left for the night, she kept on for another hour. It was only when the light got dim and she rose to switch on that she saw that Peter had stopped back, too. She saw him smiling at her, and she wished she could smile back at him, forget what Karl Kemble had asked.

'Given to you,' he had asked hatefully, 'by our young Q.S.?'

'Certainly not,' she had answered at once, but how convincing had she sounded, and how convincing could it look with Peter waiting for her like this?

Yet there had been nothing. Simply a few figures. A few figures taken from a memo that Renata had not even bothered to conceal—though ... and again Junia thought it ... she had had to *look* for it, and as things had happened she wished now she never had.

Shrugging it all off, or trying to, Junia turned to Peter, and smiled back at last.

CHAPTER TEN

THERE followed a week of hard work. Junia barely left her typewriter, and she noted that Peter's nose was seldom out of his books. She put it down to Big Brother's daily attendance, but when she remarked this once to Renata, the girl shook her head. She seemed excited, stimulated, and there was no doubt that the increased activity suited her. Her olive cheeks had become beautifully flushed, her dark eyes glittered.

'No, it's not Karl,' she denied, 'I mean it is, of course, but it's not just him. No, there's something cooking. I can feel it.'

'Cooking?' queried Junia.

'Afoot. Something discovered or on the verge of discovery. Something big.' Now the eyes were pinpoints of light.

'You mean all those little flags marching to Kingdom Come,' laughed Junia. The flags marked the signs that the geologists had noticed, the indications.

'Oh, more than that.' Renata must have suddenly remembered herself, for she corrected : 'Well, possibly, I should say, Junia. Anyway, a find of some sort. Something is always found out here. I expect we'll learn soon enough.'

'I expect so.' Junia wondered if things were always discovered like this, to the tune of bated breath and an air of near-climax, or whether this was something special.

On one of the rare occasions when she found an

opportunity to speak to Peter, Junia asked the Q.S. outright.

'There's an about-to-burst feeling, Peter—what is it? What is about to be found? Is it wolfram? Mica? Nickel? Oil? Or just old stones?' The old stones was added in fun because of Peter's shocked face.

'You don't, you simply don't ask such things, Junia,' Peter protested.

'But I'd like to know,' she persisted.

'You still don't ask.'

'Were you taught that at mining school?'

'No, but I've learned it here.'

'Then you don't know, either.'

'Junia!' he exclaimed in exasperation.

'I'm sorry, but I thought your breath might be bated, too.'

'Breath? Bated?'

'I thought you might be on the verge ... the edge. Oh, you must have noticed it, Peter. There's discovery in the air.'

'Well, yes, I have,' he admitted, 'but——'

'I understand. I also believe you. And I'm sorry I shocked you by asking. I didn't mean anything.'

She did believe Peter, she believed he knew as little as she did, but Renata, later, did not. However, that was later, and standing beside Peter now, Junia saw only his frank grey eyes and his pleasant open expression

'Junia,' he was proposing, dropping the other subject, 'we must buzz off again. I mean, when we're not so busy.'

'Yes, Peter.'

'I still have this coast trip in mind,' he said persuasively.

'Rule me out there, I'm definitely not permitted.'

During one of her encounters with Karl Kemble, Junia had mentioned Peter's proposal, and been at once, and very firmly, forbidden.

'I wouldn't think of allowing it.' Karl had frowned. 'It's too far for a woman; also we're approaching the cyclone season.'

Junia related it now to Peter.

'Yes,' he nodded, 'but I estimated that we could be there and back before the big blows happened. A cyclone always comes at the same time of year, so one can plan well ahead.'

'Not this one. No, Peter, definitely not allowed.'

Peter was disappointed, but he took it well.

'Well, you've been to the coast already,' he pointed out, 'so it's not so important to you as it is to me. Junia, it's very important to me. I feel I must go while I'm still here.'

'While you're still here ... why, did you think of leaving?'

'Mining work always entails leaving, Junia,' Peter reminded her. 'But apart from that——'

'Yes?' Junia had noticed a faint cloud on the boy's face, and she was curious.

But—'I don't know,'—was all that Peter could explain to her. 'I only know I want to see it before——'

'Before you go?'

'Yes.' Peter sounded uncertain of his reason but very certain of his desire.

In all that week not once did Junia find time to seek out Colin. It seemed incredible to her not to be able to run down the hill to him, but pressure of work kept her at her desk all day with only short meal breaks. Also Renata had asked her, from Karl Kemble, to work late at night.

At Junia's disappointed look on one occasion, Renata

had soothed: 'Your big pay envelope will be very welcome when you two take off soon, remember.'

'Yes, I suppose you're right, but I haven't seen Colin at all. He must be taking his meals at different hours.'

'Aren't we all?' sighed Renata. 'My own dear fiancé certainly believes in working you while the rush is on.'

'What kind of rush is it?' asked Junia.

'Oh, come, Junia, no doubt *Peter* has told you.'

'No.'

'Then ask him. I'd like to know myself.' A careless laugh.

'But Peter knows as much as we do.'

'Oh, really, dear, you don't believe that? The quantity surveyor?'

'Yes, I believe Peter,' Junia said, but not quite so convinced as before. She was recalling Peter's shock at her question. Shock ... or evasion? She was recalling Karl Kemble's sharp interrogation of her regarding Peter. She sighed. She hated all this sublety, deceit, innuendo. Why did such a place as this have to deal in things like that?

Junia eluded Peter that afternoon, and ran down the hill to the unit at the bottom of the row. This time she would see Colin. But nearly there, for some reason she slackened her pace. She even stood a long moment before she went to the door. For a second she thought: 'Why have I come?'

'Why have I come? Why hasn't Colin sought me out?'

Then she remembered Big Brother, and understood Colin's predicament. How could he seek her out with a hovering Karl Kemble? How could an outsider?

She crossed to Colin's front door, went to knock, then found it unlocked, so went in. The room was in semi-darkness, for it was that darkling time of evening, but it was not the half-obscurity that halted Junia, it was——

It was that drift of jasmine again. That sweetness that Colin had said was the essence of the Australian bush, but a sweetness that she firmly believed was *not*. Frowning slightly, Junia moved forward again.

Colin must have left the room only just recently, for his notes were still on the table, uncovered. Idly, Junia crossed to them. She picked them up idly, she looked incuriously at what was to be Colin's book. She knew she should feel a pride in that fact, and she reached down inside of her to find the pride, but either it was her tiredness after a week of hard work, or—or something, but she could feel nothing at all.

She examined the sheets. All she could see was a blurred column of figures, blurred in the semi-darkness. No writing at all. Wasn't that rather a curious book?

'Junia, what are you doing?'

It was the tone of the voice that startled Junia, made her drop the sheets, nothing else. It was not Colin's sudden appearance, she had expected Colin. But she had never expected Colin to speak to her like that.

She turned as her fiancé came up to the desk.

'What are you doing?' Colin asked again.

Junia looked up at him and gave an instinctive step back. She had never seen Colin looking like this before. His face was tight and drawn and his lips were thinned. His eyes were narrowed so that they were only slits of light. He put his hands on her arms, put them very roughly, and for an absurd moment Junia had the feeling he was going to shake her, or even push her. Then the moment went, for Colin as well as Junia.

'My dear, I believe I frightened you,' Colin said solicitously. 'I didn't mean to. I'd just gone out a moment and when I came back there was a figure bent

146

over my desk.'

'Me,' she pointed.

'But I couldn't see it was you, could I?'

'No—no, it's nearly dark. But who would walk in to look at what you'd written? I mean, Colin, would anyone in this place, surrounded by things that you're writing about, be that much interested in your book? Your publisher, yes, and your reading public one day, but not men on an outpost who are literally surrounded with the subject and background from morning to night.'

'You're right, of course, my sweet, but I'm a new-chum at this writing game, remember, and—well, I get a little uptight about it at times.' Colin gave a little laugh of self-deprecation and apparent embarrassment.

Colin uptight, as he put it! Colin had always been very cool, very much the master of any situation.

Junia smiled, however, and soothed: 'I think I know what you mean. I can remember going through agonies at having my essays read out in class.'

'The same,' Colin nodded. 'Fool, aren't I? Oh, my dear Junia, it's lovely to see you again.'

'It's lovely to see you, Colin. We've had our noses to the grindstone.'

'So Renata told me.'

'. . . Then you've seen Renata?'

A small silence, so small it almost did not occur.

'I have to pay my weekly sustenance bill,' reminded Colin. 'Renata naturally deals with all that.'

'Of course.' A pause. 'Colin——'

'Yes, dearest?'

'How long now? How long before we can leave?'

'But I thought you liked it. I thought the young Q.S. was taking you around and that you enjoyed this part of the world.'

'Put it that I love this part of the world but not its people.'

'Has the young Q.S. been worrying you, then?' Colin put in jovially, but somehow the faint innuendo sickened Junia. She pushed the distaste aside, though, and answered instead:

'I don't like the atmosphere here. There's no bond, no trust. Sometimes ... sometimes I even feel an enmity.'

'My dear Junia, what an imagination! It's you who should be writing my book.'

'A book of figures?'

A definite pause this time.

'So you *were* reading it?' Colin accused

'How can you read figures? Really, Colin!' Junia was aggrieved.

Colin seemed to shake himself out of something. It was the barest of movements, but when he spoke again he was his old bland self.

'Books on subjects like this can scarcely run to romantic conversations,' he reminded her.

'Nor include any purple patches,' mused Junia, sorry now she had spoken as she had.

Colin glanced sharply at her at that. Even though it was near-dark now in the room, Junia could see that sharpness in his glance.

'But when he said: 'What's the latest rumour about our own purple patches, darling?' he almost yawned as though the subject rather bored him. 'I don't mean the Salvation Jane purple but the finds underneath the Jane. There's something doing, isn't there? Have you heard?'

'No.'

'Then, sweet, if you do, please let Yours Truly know.'

'What for?' she asked.

'Why, to put in my book, of course. It would make a grand last chapter. Now don't look at me like that, by the time my manuscript is typed, accepted and published, all Australia will know whatever there is to be known here, and my information will be very old hat. Oh, no, my Junia, you would be divulging nothing.'

'I suppose not,' Junia agreed, 'if I knew. But I don't.'

She went back to her previous theme, the reason, she prompted herself, she really had come down here.

'When can we go, Colin? Can't you finish the book in Sydney?'

'No, I'm afraid I can't, Junia. I plan a really good finale, and to have that I must be on hand right to the last full stop. But it won't be long now, dear, I promise you that. Meanwhile try to bear with me, and if any pertinent bits and pieces come to hand, tell me. It will make our exit all the quicker, and that's what you want—what we both want. But please be patient now, dearest. After all, you came here of your own accord, remember, I didn't bring you. I mean' ... at a hurt look in her face ... 'all I ever wanted to do was make good for you and then get back to you again. Oh, I do love you here, my darling, but my original plans have not altered. I still want a good home in a civilised city with you. I must have that.'

'Yes,' Junia agreed dully. She kissed him goodbye almost mechanically, in her absorption not noticing his equally mechanical kiss, then she went back up the hill, knowing as she did so that she wanted no civilised city, that she wanted—wanted Far-Off.

The work slackened to a more normal pace with the departure of Karl Kemble and some men of his to some exploratory field for several days, but the heady air of excitement did not.

With more time on her hands Junia listened to Renata when the girl urged her to take some days off from the hours she had accumulated, and join Peter in the invitations he was always pressing on her, for Peter, too, had not spared himself and now had collected a considerable helping of leisure. 'After all, you do have Colin's blessing,' Renata pointed out.

'Yes, and Big Brother's.' At an inquiring look from Renata, Junia told her how Peter on the last occasion had reported no disapproval from his boss concerning their jaunts.

'No, Karl is very fair,' nodded Renata. 'For instance, he never minded me befriending your fiancé, even though he couldn't bring himself to be nice to Colin.'

'And I must always be grateful to you for that, Renata,' said Junia dutifullly. 'Are all places like this so distrustful? I had a friend who worked at a hydro project and it was entirely friendly.'

'But then water isn't nickel, oil, uranium, what-have-you, is it?' laughed Renata.

'No, but I know which I would prefer in a desert.'

'Well, you won't be here long to worry about that, will you? Not if you play your cards right.'

'That sounds—well——' Junia began.

'Plotting? It isn't, though. There might be need for buttoned lips among the staff, but Colin ... well, he merely wants material to finish his book.'

'Yes, he told me.'

'He just can't wait to take you back south with him, Junia.' Renata sighed feelingly. 'Oh, dear, I am going to miss you too!'

'We haven't gone yet,' Junia pointed out smilingly.

'But I feel you will. I feel you will help Colin in this final difficult chapter.'

'I?' Junia questioned.

'You know what I mean, dear. You could ask Peter for a few helpful pointers.'

'Peter knows nothing—I told you.'

'Then you could ask Peter to try to discover ... undoubtedly the poor smitten boy would do anything for you ... and from that Colin could get his chapter down in all the heat of the moment that's so important in a book. No, Junia' ... as Junia went to say something ... 'it's useless for him to try to write later from notes. Do you, for instance, think you could describe a sunrise in the middle of the afternoon?'

'No,' giggled Junia, 'not when you put it like that.'

'I do. And, dear, don't think that anything that you might hand on could *matter*,' Renata went on. 'Colin was telling me he will be relying on you to type the top copy once the two of you are back in Sydney, and even if you were a very rapid typist that would take a considerable time. Any news would be stale economically by then. And' ... an arch look ... 'you're not really rapid, are you, pet?'

'No. Oh, I wish——' Junia began.

'That you were?'

'... Yes.' It was not the truth. Junia was wishing that she did not have to do anything for Colin, wishing that Colin simply felt as she did, that he wanted to stay here regardless of any book. Stay for ever.

Peter was delighted when Junia told him she would come out again, and at once took out a small pad in which he had jotted down any place of interest he had heard mentioned.

'Mary Miranda,' he read to Junia. 'The Rosendo Mission. One-Tree Hollow. The Indian Ocean.' He glanced slyly at Junia at that last.

'You know I can't do that one, Peter—anyway, you've

enough to fill our accumulated hours and more, I should say.'

One-Tree Hollow proved just that, a saucer in the vast flatness of the desert with exactly one tree in it. The remarkable thing was that it was a palm tree. Here in the wastes a palm tree lifted its tender green fronds to form a single oasis. Peter related to Junia what he had gleaned about One-Tree Hollow and particularly about the variety of palm.

'You've heard of Palm Valley?' he asked.

'I've even visited it, Peter.' Junia shut her eyes a moment in enchanted memory of that valley beyond Alice Springs that she had seen some years ago, untouched by civilisation, revealing by its giant red sandstone rocks circling, its proud soaring palms, that it was not just the land of yesterday but the very beginning.

'There were rock pools,' she marvelled to Peter, 'trickling water. But' ... looking around her ... 'what connection has One-Tree Hollow with it?'

'Perhaps none, but it's suspected that once here, too, was a green oasis.'

'And only this tree survives. How does it, Peter?'

'Something underground,' he shrugged. 'There are more rivers beneath the earth than on top of the earth in this crazy country.'

They went down to Rosendo Mission. It was a Spanish Benedictine order, and went back to the eighteen-hundreds.

'Australia was very young then,' mused Peter.

The good fathers, Father Sebastian and Father Basil, welcomed them, made them sample their desert wine, try their monastery bread.

'The men,' said Peter as the drove back to Far-Off, 'say they're a wonderful order. They only help, they never intrude. The natives are encouraged to hold their own rituals. Mary Miranda tomorrow, Junia?'

'Well——'

'Look, you must have accumulated that much overtime. I know I have.'

He was tempting her, and Junia told him so.

'Then be tempted,' Peter persuaded.

In all this time neither Renata nor Colin had asked Junia about her outings with Peter, and for that Junia was grateful. Possibly if they had, she would *not* have questioned Peter as she did the next day at Mary Miranda.

Mary Miranda ... no one knew how the place had become that ... was one of the unexpected chasms that the inside sometimes surprised you with, suddenly out of the barren waste would rise walls of red rock, forming an amphitheatre in which marvellous scenes were shown.

To witness the climax of colour, Peter said, one had to climb to a position where the sun would arrow down between the walls of the rock, and exactly at full sun, which would be midday, the miracle would be enacted.

It was enacted. If Junia thought there was colour before, now she drew her breath sharply in wonder and disbelief. Such flame, such flaunting scarlet, such poppy crimson could not exist, she doubted. But the gold she could not doubt, for it spilled everywhere. There was not a rock, not a stone, not a gibber, not even a small pebble that did not change to glittering gilt.

'Midas country,' Junia claimed.

'Yes, Scrooge would have sat down and counted till doomsday.'

'And Big Brother?' It was out before Junia realised it.

Peter laughed back at Junia. He was as drunk with

153

the colour as she was. 'How did you guess?' he teased. 'Because I told you about a lone prospector with a dolly pot?'

'Then the secret is not mica, wolfram, nickel, the mundane rest, but gold?'

'Hush, Junia! When it comes to gold even a leaf will gossip it.' Peter said it extravagantly, still carried away with the glitter, with the radiant largesse.

'No, sing it,' corrected Junia gaily. 'That golden flood is a singing, not a gossiping colour.' She had completely forgotten her pertinent question to Peter in the almost unbelievable beauty of full noon over Mary Miranda. Peter had forgotten, too.

The glitter of it all remained with Junia on the way back to Far-Off ... but the pertinence did not. When she encountered Renata walking down the corridor of the hostel she tossed gaily to her: 'Gold, Renata. Shining gold!'

She was still aflame with colour.

It was only when she was changing for dinner from her dusty desert jeans that Junia realised her possible indiscretion. She had called something to Renata in passing, and anyone could have heard. What had Peter said? 'Even a leaf will gossip the message of gold.'

She felt very disgusted with herself. No harm would come of it, but it had not been a good thing to do. She would speak to Renata at the evening meal.

But Renata was not at the evening meal, either that or she had come earlier. It was the same with Colin, and Peter only dashed in for a bite, explaining to Junia in passing that Big Brother was back from the field and that he wanted some immediate work from his Q.S.

'Didn't you tell him you've been at the grindstone too much for that?' she asked.

'No, I didn't, Junia, because I want to be very impressive, and after Mr Kemble is duly impressed, I want to ask him can I go off to the coast tomorrow. Yes, tomorrow. I've been warned that it won't be long now before the big blows blow. I'll do this stint for Mr Kemble at once, then put it to him to let me push off in the early morning. I feel he'll agree. He's quite eager for anyone to look around his beloved country—I only wish you could come, too.'

'No hope, Peter. So you'll go in the small hours?'

'Piccaninny daylight, if you happen to change your mind, Junia.'

'You really mean if Mr Kemble changes his mind about me.'

'Well, he'd always be reasonable.'

... Would he? Junia wondered as she gathered her meal from the hatch and took it back to the table. Would Karl Kemble ever be reasonable?

She found herself watching for him. If he was back he must come in for a meal. But although Junia extended her own meal to three coffees, Karl Kemble did not come, and at last Junia rose and went out.

With Peter working, she had no one to talk to. That sounded absurd when down the hill was the man she was going to marry, but she knew that if she visited Colin, though he would greet her affectionately, he would also greet her anxiously, anxious for her to go and leave him to his book again.

She felt oddly disturbed, she could not have said why. She went to her room and sat on her bed and tried to analyse her mood. She had been happy out in the bush with Peter, it had only been when she had returned that she had felt depressed like this. What had intruded? She tried to feel her way back.

It did not take her long to pinpoint her uneasiness.

It all had come when she had called carelessly to Renata:

'Gold. Shining gold!'

She had been foolish, unforgivably so. She knew the cardinal rule in a place like this and she had broken the rule. Well, it was done now, and luckily no harm done with it. Junia found a paperback and lay down and read.

She actually read for an hour before she realised she was making no sense of the printed word. She put the book down and wandered restlessly round the room.

She went out to the passage to see if there was a light under Renata's door, in which case she intended suggesting coffee and a chat. The room was in darkness.

She went down the 'convenient' staircase and looked down the hill to Colin's. His digs also were in darkness. She knew he had been working very long hours, so probably he was having an early night. She came back to her room and decided to do the same herself: to go to bed early.

She went and showered, then came back to her room, read, or tried to read for a while, then put out the light. Two hours afterwards she was tossing and turning unhappily, and she knew she would never sleep tonight, nor, the guilty way she was feeling, tomorrow night or the night after, unless she cleared her conscience.

Careless talk! She called it that as she dressed again and crossed the road to the office. She had looked through the window and seen that a light was on, and a light at such an hour could only mean one person: Big Brother. Karl Kemble would be furious when she told him that she had spoken louder than she should, she would be lectured soundly, probably punished by overtime, or even a penalty in her pay, but he would know, as she did, that she had spoken safely to his *fiancée*, and in the end, though censured, she would have an untroubled heart again and at least be able to sleep once more. That, anyhow, was how Junia thought.

She had reached the office by this time, and she tapped at once on the door.

'Yes?' The interrogative was sharp, rather unnecessarily so, Junia thought.

'Junia West, Mr Kemble.'

'What do you want?'

What did she want? Junia hesitated, her determination rapidly diminishing.

'Nothing,' she called, 'just nothing. I simply noticed your light and——' The last word was spoken inside the pre-fab, for the man had opened the door and literally flung her within.

'Really——!' Junia burst out.

'Yes, really, Miss West. You can't go knocking on a door then fobbing me off with "Nothing", not at midnight, and then expect it to come off. What *did* you knock for?'

'Nothing.'

'You said that before and you weren't convincing. That's why I hauled you inside. Now what is it you want to tell me?'

'Well, I can answer one thing,' said Junia angrily, 'it was not welcome back.'

'I can well imagine that.' His voice was thin. 'And yet' ... curiously ... 'you still knocked on the door. Did you feel lonely suddenly? Feel in need of something that obviously your fiancé down the road hasn't the time nor the inclination to——' He did not finish it. Junia, more angry than she could ever remember, had reached up and caught him a stinging blow across the cheek.

He had hold of her wrist at once, and it was a tight ruthless hold.

'You'll be sorry about that,' he growled.

'Never!'

'We'll see. Now how about a little truth, Miss West, why have you really come?'

Junia stood silent.

'If it was not to welcome me back, if it was not to——' He smiled mock-archly.

'It was not,' she inserted quickly.

'Then what?'

'It's nothing. I'll go now.'

'Not until you tell me. Good lord, what sort of fool do you take me for? You could have been knocking on the door in the chance I wasn't here and you could come in and snoop to your heart's content.'

'I have no key and I don't snoop,' she said coldly.

'Then what in heaven do you do or have done?'

'I—I was a little indiscreet,' she faltered. 'It worried me. I couldn't sleep until I told you.'

'I'm no father confessor. Wait till you go out to the Rosendo Monastery.'

'We went there through the week.'

'Then why didn't you confess your misdemeanours to Father Sebastian or Father Basil?'

Junia could have stamped her foot at him. She cried angrily: 'It wasn't anything like that, it was—a different indiscretion. I talked carelessly about this place, and I know that's something you don't do.'

'You're quite right, you don't do it. Whom did you talk to?'

'Peter.' She went to add: 'Afterwards to Renata,' but he had turned away in obvious uninterest.

'Anything else?' He asked it unimportantly, so Junia took it unimportantly.

'No,' she said.

'Well then, you've duly confessed,' he shrugged it off.

'Thank you, I feel easier now.' She turned to go.

'Wait!' he ordered. 'You're not getting off that light.'

'What do you mean?'

'You've salved your conscience ... for sleep's sake, so I think I'll salve mine ... for my own.'

'And what have you done, Mr Kemble?'

'Pretended?' He made a question of his answer.

'We all pretend.' Junia was trying to step away from the man, there was something intentional in his face, something she knew she could not handle.

But before she could withdraw, he was handling *her*. He had her in his arms in a way that Junia never had been held in anyone's arms, and certainly not Colin's. Eyes to eyes, for she could not avoid Karl Kemble's eyes. Lips to lips. Breath-close. Deliberately, as though savouring it, he kissed her, kissed her softly, quietly, then fiercely, hungrily. There was no withdrawing from him, no resisting.

'So you were an indiscreet girl,' he said in her ear.

'Never again,' she tried to fume at him, 'not after this,' but it was useless, he had her imprisoned too tightly.

'And what about your pretence, Mr Kemble?' she managed to ask him breathlessly.

'My pretence? Well, I pretended it was the other way about.'

'The other way about?'

'That I was Brent,' he said, and again his lips came down. 'Or should I say that you were Renata?' He kissed her again.

'Let me go, please,' she begged, 'you're hurting me.'

'And will keep on hurting you until you understand.

Why don't you understand, Junia? Why don't you even try?'

'You employ me to work, not understand, Mr Kemble. Also you don't rule me.'

'I do rule you, Junia, have no two thoughts about that. You'll do as I say. If you don't I'll——'

'Yes?'

'I'll make you more sorry for yourself than you are now.' He smiled thinly. 'In novels a man adds: "That's a promise, not a threat," but mine is all threat. Understand?'

'No.'

'I think you do, though. I think you realise you will have to obey me.' He made a joke of it, but the levity did not reach his compelling eyes.

'Obey——!' Junia was choked up now with indignation and disgust.

A breeze suddenly stirred the pages on his desk, and quick as a cat he turned. He was very much on the alert just now, Junia thought. But the movement had given her a chance to escape. She was out of the office and across the road in a flash.

There were a dozen things she could have been angry about ... his rough handling, his innuendo, his embrace, his censure, his—— But most infuriating of all she found his arrogant authority.

'I do rule you,' he had said. 'You'll do as I say.'

She had reached her room now and closed the door.

'I won't. I won't. I won't be ruled!' She said it to the walls. But how to prove it to him? How to defy that impossible man?

Then it came to her. The forbidden journey to the coast tomorrow, permitted for Peter but forbidden for her. ——

I'm going, Junia knew. Colin will be intent on his

160

work, he won't mind, but he ... Big Brother ... She almost laughed aloud in triumph.

She found an overnight bag she had been given by Renata and threw in a few essential things. No need to worry about sleeping in too late for piccaninny daylight because she intended sitting at the window for it to make sure. If she grew tired on the journey Peter would not mind if she dozed.

Around the same time that Karl Kemble had taken her to watch for the morning star, Junia left the hostel and walked to the garages where Peter left his wagon.

He was there already, and because it was the easiest thing to do, Junia just said directly: 'I'm coming, too, if you'll have me.'

'If I'll have you——' Peter's eyes were shining in the dark. 'But Mr Kemble——'

'Gave his blessing—last night. Oh, do hurry, Peter, I can't wait to be off.'

Peter needed no second bidding. Within five minutes they had left the project and set north-west.

CHAPTER ELEVEN

WHAT had taken Karl and Junia only an hour would take Peter in his wagon many hours. Even keeping up a steady pace, a difficult task in terrain like this, allowing no detours to examine something that might interest them, Peter told Junia they could not hope to arrive at the coast until dusk.

'There will be a hotel, won't there?' Junia asked a little uneasily; she was not regretting her impulsive action, but she wanted to be reassured about that. A night under the stars with Peter did not dismay her, but she knew someone else who would not be so tolerant, even though she had spent more than one night with him. But then there had been Jimmy as well, Jimmy tucked up under the table-top, needing no padded bag. Junia smiled in memory.

Peter did not see the smile, he was too intent on the track. He answered her question seriously.

'Of course there'll be accommodation. Mostly these places attract the unmarried employee, and the bachelors are housed in hostels or hotels, and either of those will do us.'

'Suppose they're full?'

'They'll find room. Ever heard of western hospitality?'

Yes, she had. Out on the track with Karl Kemble, but Junia did not say so to Peter.

'Don't worry,' he was telling her, 'you won't be sleeping in the car.'

'Or on the beach,' she suggested. 'You're quite excited

162

about that beach, aren't you, Peter?'

'How did you guess?' smiled Peter boyishly. 'Yes, I'm very excited. Ever since I came up here I've wanted to complete a journey, a journey I privately call my Coast-to-Coast. It's a big country, Junia; I've stood looking at the Pacific Ocean many times and now it will give me a thrill to stand and look at the Indian. It's—well, I can't explain it properly, except that it's something that I must do, that I have to do, and that's why——'

'Yes, Peter?'

'Well, that's why I came, though I *didn't* get an OK from Big Brother as I told you. Yes, that's true.' Peter took his eyes off the rutted track a moment to look ruefully at Junia.

'You didn't get an OK?' she gasped.

'Well, you didn't, either, for all your innocent expression as you told me that lie, you didn't get it because Karl Kemble wouldn't have given it. Too near the cyclone season, he told me.'

'But——' she began.

'But I still had to come, cyclone or summer breeze.' Peter's mouth set obstinately. 'It was one of those things, those compulsions. You must have had them.'

'Yes . . . yes, I have had them.' She had had one when she had come up here after Colin. She was thoughtful for a while. 'But if Big Bro—if Mr Kemble wouldn't permit you, how are you here now, Peter?'

'Because he doesn't know. Oh, he's aware I'm taking my accumulated leave and looking round the country, *his* country, for he's all for that. But not for the coast, Junia, not at this time of year.'

'I wouldn't have thought it of you, Peter,' Junia told him in mock reproof, 'you get on so well with Mr Kemble.'

'Very well. I like him very much. But I wanted to do

163

this, Junia, this Coast-to-Coast of mine. I suppose it's become an obsession, a commitment. I've never travelled, yet always yearned to, but it seemed it wasn't to be for people like me.'

'People like you?' she questioned.

Peter didn't answer that. 'But now it's changed,' he went on, 'I mean it will be changed, I'll have crossed a big country.' His hands tightened on the steering wheel until the knuckle bones showed white. He was very moved. Presently he composed himself and accused Junia affectionately: 'Fellow conspirator!'

'Well, not actually, I came mainly out of spite.'

'Spite?' Peter looked at her.

'Last night Big Brother' ... she did not correct herself this time ... 'became very much the master.'

'He is the master,' he said reasonably.

'Not of me.'

'Well, he's the boss. Isn't that the same?'

'There's a difference.'

'A subtle one. But go on, Junia.'

'He gave me orders. *Orders*, Peter. His actual words were: "I rule you. You'll do as I say".'

'And you didn't like that? I thought girls went for the masterful type.'

Junia dealt with the second statement first.

'I don't go for the masterful type, and if I liked the idea of being ruled, would I be here?'

'Did he directly forbid this?' asked Peter.

'Not last night, but previously. No, he just made a general statement that——'

'That he cracked the whip?'

'Exactly. So I went back to the hostel and thought "How can I defy him"? '

'And here you are?'

'Here I am.'

'I wouldn't have thought it of you, Junia.' Peter used the same mock reproof words as she had to him— But he did not add: 'You get on well with Mr Kemble,' for he must know that she did not.

Confessions over, they both lapsed into a comfortable silence, Peter's quiet very necessary if he was to keep up a reasonable pace over such a difficult track, Junia's silence because of the country they travelled, every turn of it bringing something different, a new colour, a new magnificence, for it was near-magnificent terrain.

For all its dreamlike beauty, there was still something substantial, strong and everlasting in it, in the soaring purple walls of rock that rose intermittently, in the blood-red indentations of earth stretching endlessly west towards that sea that Peter had set his heart on, in the lupin distances and the painted blue skies.

They drank from a flask and ate a few biscuits around noon, not even seeking out some old wurlie in which to dabble their fingers and toes, for it was very hot now, not even finding a bark tree for shade, simply eating the snack quickly in the car, then setting off again.

During the afternoon they saw a dust cloud far in the horizon and knew it would be teams channelling their way across to the nearest road trains, for there was no Bitumen out here on which to speed a thirty-six-wheeler, and overlanding had to be undertaken to the nearest highway.

The country was always different ... lunar-bare for miles, arid, even hostile, then suddenly blossoming into a garden. There were many old diggings, evidently relinquished as the digger lost heart and left the mullock behind him like a violent scar on the already violent red earth.

Mid-afternoon they met their first car. They slackened pace to wave, but the car from the coast direction stopped altogether and the driver got out. Peter stopped as well.

'You're going the wrong way, aren't you?' the driver called.

'Port Simon?'

'Yes, man, but folk aren't going there today, they're coming away.'

'The cyclone?' queried Junia.

'Not quite yet, but they're on the alert. Name of Godfrey, if you please. Women's Lib have protested and they're using male names now as well.'

'But Godfrey came the last time.' Junia remembered reading about Godfrey, he had not turned out as fierce as had been anticipated.

'But he never quite bowed out. Radar Cyclone Warning has reported a strong possibility of a re-curve of Godfrey, and when I left Port Simon, Godfrey was parallel to the coast. Anyway, a blue warning is out.'

Because of some stubborn reason Peter did not ask it, Junia inquired: 'What is a "blue warning"?'

'A twenty-four-hour standby. I was at Darwin for Tracy, and that was enough for me. I'm getting out.'

'Well, you seem to be the only one.' Peter spoke at last.

'You'll meet them,' the man promised, and went back to his car.

'Peter, do you think——' Junia began as they set off again.

'No, I don't,' Peter said before she could finish what she had to ask. 'No, Junia. Anyway, I read before I came that this one, this Godfrey, has no well-defined eye, in fact all they expect, even in a re-curve, is a good blow.' He set his lips obstinately. He was very keen to get to that coast, Junia judged.

166

They were hailed again during the afternoon. One man leaning perilously out of his car called to them that Godfrey had increased its pace from eleven kilometres an hour to eighteen.

'But only out at sea,' Peter shouted back.

'Yes, but he has a big diameter.'

After they had left the warning motorists, Peter said to Junia: 'There may be an increase, but no one can ever say for sure where a cyclone will strike.'

'Peter——'

But a glance at Peter's face stopped Junia. She could see that whatever she protested would make no difference. Anyway, *did* she want to stop him? The fat, she shrugged, was now well and truly in the fire. They were too far advanced to turn back to Far-Off, they would never make it by tonight, so if they were to be absent without leave, they might as well get something out of it. She said as much to Peter, and he smiled gratefully and told her he had depended on her to say that.

A few more cars passed, all waving, all shouting warnings, but Junia could not have blamed Peter for looking disbelieving; the sky was a bright flag blue now, no mares' tails of clouds that usually ushered in a big blow, only innocuous balls of white cottonwool. It was peaceful and even sleepy.

The first indication came abruptly. A sullen grey patch appeared literally from nowhere, and even as they watched it turned black and spread across as though it was being poured from a giant ink-bottle.

Within minutes ... even seconds, it seemed ... day became night. Peter put on the lights and started the windscreen wipers, for the first drops of rain had begun. They were not drops for long, soon they were drumming fiendishly down on the roof of the car, slashing

167

at the bonnet. It was much worse when the first blow of wind started, for it changed the rain to a horizontal direction, and the wet beat against the windscreen so intensely there was no visibility.

But they struggled onward, since there seemed little use to do anything else. Peter just crawled now, and there was no question of his reaching Port Simon by dusk. Dusk—that was a joke. Already it was darker than night.

Then as abruptly as they had come, the winds paused, the drops of rain only fell intermittently.

'It's over,' said Junia in vast relief. 'As cyclones go, Godfrey was no great guns.'

'Yes,' said Peter happily. 'Now I know we *were* doing the right thing. For a few moments, Junia, I thought——'

He hurried the car now, not even slackening to wave back to more cars coming from the opposite direction. Some of the drivers called out, but in their speed they didn't hear a word. They were both excited, even a little intoxicated, almost hysterically glad to be on their way again. Probably, anyhow, it was only a jocund remark the motorists made about the changeable weather.

This lasted for perhaps an hour, and then, this time with not even a sullen cloud for a warning, Godfrey recycled and really struck.

They were passing through some low timber terrain at the moment, but at once the timber was levelled to the ground, in many cases, Junia saw, shaved right off. She felt sure that the car temporarily rose in the air. It righted itself again, and Peter, pale now, kept going, no doubt feeling safer driving against the wind than with it, knowing, too, that there would be no shelter in these sparse woods.

They went painfully on uprooted bushes banging against the car's body, gibber and stones hitting up at them and making a sound like discharging metal.

Now the rain did not just obliterate everything for them, it slashed, screamed and tried to cut at them through the protective glass. Every now and then it would take a breathing space to get ready for another demon attack, and that, Junia thought, was the worst of all. She found herself holding her breath in dread, and she knew Peter was doing the same.

But still he crawled on, how Junia did not know, but it seemed the only thing to try to do; there was no possible shelter and with such a shrieking gale they had to fight it out or be windborne to heaven knew where.

'We'll keep on,' Peter gritted to Junia, 'while the glass still stands between us and the demons. Oh, Junia, Junia, what have I put you in for?'

'I came myself,' insisted Junia, 'and anyway, it can't last for ever.'

'They have lasted for three or four days.'

'But not at this tempo.'

'No . . . but the question is how long can we last?'

'It might race out as it raced in,' she pointed out.

'I hope so. I pray so.'

'Everything will be all right,' Junia assured him, hoping and praying already. She felt she had to say that, had to put her hand quickly and comfortingly over Peter's hand. His pale face had alarmed her. She knew, in spite of her assuring words, that he was blaming himself in this. 'Tomorrow,' she promised, 'will be another day.'

She said it just as the window splintered in front of them from the impact of a torn-up tree, not a big tree, there were no big trees here, but dashing against the glass the impact was shattering. The car swerved and came to a halt against some rock. Junia lurched forward and bumped her head, for the glass had only shattered on the driver's side.

The driver's side ...

Junia turned and peered through the darkness at Peter. Even this close she could not see him, everthing was too black, she could not see the wound which she knew had been inflicted.

She would not have known about the wound had she not felt the blood. Following the impact, instinctively she had held her fingers to him, and she had encountered the thicker than rain wetness ... and she had known. Known that he had been hurt.

Yet he evidently did not know himself. He said jokingly: 'I say, Junia, that was a real mean trick, wasn't it?' and because she still had the feel of his blood on her fingers, Junia listened for ... and heard ... a telltale slur already in his voice. She knew he was in a bad way.

'Yes,' she answered as normally as she could, 'a mean trick. Peter, are you——'

'All right? I'm fine. A bit cut about, I would say, but nothing serious. And you, darling?'

She started a little at that 'darling'. Peter always had looked at her in a way that could leave her no possible doubts as to how he felt, but he had never used an endearment.

'About the same as you,' she lied to him, for she had no cuts since her section of the glass had not broken. 'But,' she added cheerfully, 'we won't be able to tell properly until it gets lighter.'

'That will be tomorrow morning. It's night now.' Peter sighed. 'So near and yet so far.'

'Your Coast-to-Coast?'

'Yes, Junia. I still keep thinking about that. I suppose you'd say I was crazy.'

'No, I wouldn't, Peter. It's only to be expected. You told me you'd never travelled.'

'Not at all. I was brought up in a home. Yes, an orphanage—I was an orphan. My entire travelling was across to the school during the week, and to church on Sunday. Oh, the people were good, but I had this feeling——'

'Itchy feet?' Junia made herself banter.

'More—well, closed in. Sort of—girt. Unfulfilled. I' ... humbly, a little embarrassed ... 'turned out fairly bright, so they, the Board, took pains with me and put me through advanced classes in the city, so at least I travelled there. Then later, education finished, exams passed, before I could look around, or book a ticket, or hitch a ride, or—or *something*, Junia, Karl Kemble had me up here. Oh, I was very pleased, very proud, but——'

His voice was becoming slower, more difficult now, but Junia knew he would not be aware of that.

'So what's your worry?' she asked him. 'You've waited this long, so what's another night?'

'Exactly.' But he had to say it twice to enunciate it. 'Especially with you beside me. You do want to see it, too, don't you?'

'The ocean, Peter? Your Coast-to-Coast? Yes, I do.'

'Then we'll stand together and just gaze at it. It will be a good start for our life with each other. For we are going to be like that, aren't we, Junia?'

Junia paused, but only for the smallest of seconds.

'Yes, we're going to be together,' she said firmly.

'I love you—you know that.'

'Yes.'

'And you love me?'

The tears were pouring down Junia's cheeks now. She was inexperienced in anything like this, but she knew quite surely that there was going to be no morning for Peter, no bright ocean, no Coast-to-Coast, no beginning of a new life.

'Yes, I love you, Peter.'

'For a while I thought——' he muttered.

'Yes?'

'Karl Kemble. Big Brother.'

'Who wants a brother?' She tried to make a joke of it. It did not reach her just then that Peter had not said Colin.

She tried to see Peter's face, and once she believed she did. Whether the darkness lifted for a moment or not, she still believed she saw his face. She was happily surprised at first, it was barely marked, and there appeared only one wound. Quite a small wound. It was in the temple, and it wasn't bleeding very much now, it seemed to have congealed.

She groped for a cushion she had seen earlier and put it under his head.

'No,' he objected gallantly ... and only Junia would ever know the gallantry ... 'you.'

'Silly,' she responded, 'I have one already.'

But she didn't have one, nor did she want one. She was almost kneeling across Peter now, trying *not* to recognise the unmistakable signs, the blurring speech, the rapidly stiffening lips that even the obscurity could not obscure. Then, breath-close, she tried *not* to see ... yet saw ... the eyes begin to glaze.

But she knew, anyway, that Peter could see nothing any more, that he wouldn't have seen it even if the darkness had lifted to daylight, she knew he was beyond it. Almost beyond sound as well, for when he spoke again it was only that, bare sound, scarcely discernible.

'Jun-ia——'

'Peter?'

'I-love-you.'

'I love you,' Junia said, and she found his face and kissed it.

She did not know when Peter died. Probably it was some time afterwards as she still sat on thinking about the sea he had not reached and never would, and about a little un-belonging boy who had grown into a man, a man who had wanted to buy a ticket to somewhere, or hitch a ride, or——

Coast-to-Coast, Junia thought.

It could have been as soon as when he had said: 'I-love-you' that he had died, or it could have been when she told him back:

'I love you.'

For she *had* loved Peter, loved him in a way reserved for the Peters in the world, loved him very much.

She wished she had discouraged him from coming here. He would have come regardless, but if only she had persuaded him not to come just yet ...

If ... if ... if ... If only this night would end and she would find it had all been a dream, that they were back at Far-Off, that nothing had happened. She closed her eyes in pain. She had no fear of the still figure now beside her, he had been her gentle companion in life, so how could she have a fear afterwards? Besides, perhaps in the morning ... yes, in the morning ...

In the morning the wind had abated. The sky was still grey, but the blue was fast showing through. Everything was in a shambles, but not hopelessly so. They had left the road, but the track was still able to be regained, and, Junia judged, still negotiable. Everything seemed *not* as bad, *not* as disastrous as she had thought, everything ... except——

Except Peter. Peter had died. Died from a small sharp splinter of flying glass.

He had died last night where everything else had survived.

Except Peter.

CHAPTER TWELVE

Junia stumbled out to the road and waited for something to come along. From either direction would do, it did not matter so long as there was someone to halt and ask for help.

She was quite dry-eyed as she stood by the track. She felt nothing at all. No—that was wrong, she was experiencing an awful hollowness within her, a kind of bottomless pit. Yet actually she suffered no pain of amputation because of Peter, instead it was almost as though she was watching all this take place and that she was playing no active part.

That was how the driver of the coast-bound truck saw her, white, drained—yet curiously detached as though she did not belong. Shocked, he summed up.

He put her gently in the cabin, then went across to Peter's car. When he came back, he said: 'I'll take you to Port Simon and you can get in touch from there.' With an awkward attempt at conversation he added: 'It was quite a blow.'

'Yes,' Junia said.

Afterwards Junia could not remember giving any names, any location, and yet she must have. She was placed in a hotel ... 'Don't worry, Junia, you won't be sleeping in the car,' Peter had assured her ... and within an hour, Junia still sitting numbly where she had been put, Karl Kemble walked in.

She flinched when she saw him, but he pretended not to notice it.

'I flew across at once,' he told her. 'Will you feel fit enough to start back soon?'

'Back where?'

'Far-Off.'

'Far-Off?' she echoed.

'Yes, you came from there. Remember?'

'I remember. With Peter. Peter?'

'He's dead.' He did not say it harshly for all the brevity, he simply stated it.

'I know, but—what about Peter?'

'We'll decide that later.'

'No, now. *Now*. You'll leave him here, won't you? It's what he came for, you see—Coast-to-Coast. It's a big country. He stood and looked at the Pacific Ocean and now he wants to look at the Indian. You see, he never went anywhere before. He didn't belong.' She stopped, even in her numbness knowing she must be making no sense.

Yet the man understood 'Go on, Junia,' he said.

'No, that's all. Just leave him.' It was all Junia could think to say, to appeal. She was not aware that her eyes were saying it, her quivering mouth, her upturned palms as well.

'We'll leave him, then,' Karl Kemble agreed. He waited a moment, then asked: 'Now will you come?'

They were driven to the small air-strip. The man behind the wheel showed them what damage had been done, and it was surprisingly moderate. 'Godfrey was good to us,' he said.

Junia turned away.

Within minutes they were in Karl's Cherokee and flying east. Neither spoke during the journey, nor on the next journey, after they had left the plane, into the base.

176

Karl pulled up at the hostel and came round to the passenger's seat.

'Go in, run a bath, afterwards lie down,' he ordered. 'You'll feel a little better.'

'Perhaps Renata——' Junia was thinking wistfully that Renata might come and sit beside her for a few minutes, let her cry to her as one does cry with a woman, a different grief than with a man, but Karl Kemble came in almost violently:

'*No!*'

'But——' Junia longed for comfort. She could almost have put her hands out for it. But how could she ever tell this hard man how much she needed it? How could she ever confide in Karl Kemble? But perhaps Colin——

She paused. Suddenly it had come forcibly to Junia that during all her distress not once had she thought of Colin. It also came forcibly to her that only because everything else ... everyone else ... had failed her she was thinking of him now. All the same, he was someone to go to, to put her arms out to, to——

'I'll see Colin,' she said.

'*No.*'

'Oh, I'm aware I'm dirty, dishevelled, but Colin won't mind.'

'You're very right, he won't mind. But you won't go, Junia, instead you'll go inside. You'll do as I say. I'll give you a little time, then I'll come in to see that you are obeying me.' Obeying him! She recalled that night in his office and the same authority he had showed then, how she had hated him for it, how, later, she had run down to Peter.

'Is that a promise or a threat?' That was another thing he had said, but as soon as she retorted it, Junia could not believe she had answered it, not at a moment

177

like this. She glanced up, and saw from his hard face that she had.

'Go,' he told her.

She turned and ran up the stairs, then down the corridor. Her head had started to ache and her eyes were burning. She could not have said *why* she went past her own door to Renata's, it was certainly not in rebellion, not consciously, anyway. Possibly, she thought afterwards, in her blind awareness she simply mistook Renata's door for hers.

She turned the handle. If the door had resisted she would have known at once she was turning the wrong knob, for she never bothered to lock up at any time, but Renata never failed. It had intrigued Junia on many occasions to see how seriously Renata regarded security. Always she checked, then double-checked.

But the door did not resist, and, still unaware, she went in.

For a moment she simply stood and stared. Not because it was the wrong room but because it was—an empty room. Oh, the bed and furniture were still there, but it was empty, empty of the things that make a room a room. Empty, too, of its owner.

There was nothing on the dressing table top. The doors of the wardrobe were flung open and there were no clothes there. There were no books. No lipstick, cigarettes, matches, magazines. No cosmetics. No calendar with outlined dates and jotted notes. There was simply nothing, except——

Except a faint yet persistent scent.

Junia came further into the room, and the scent grew stronger, sweeter, more positive. Jasmine. Yes, it was jasmine. The same pervading jasmine that she had sensed down at Colin's, but more actual here, as though this was its source. Jasmine in Renata's room, in Renata's abandoned room, for it must be abandoned to be bare like this. There had been jasmine, too, at Colin's house when first she had gone there ... there had been a drift of it whenever she had gone since.

She put her hand on the back of a chair to steady herself. She was thinking a lot of things much too fast. There had been jasmine in the room she had taken over from Renata, the room that Renata had insisted she have, and she understood why now. Renata might have moved, but the perfume lingered on, for jasmine was synonymous with Renata.

Now an impact was hitting Junia. Renata ... Colin. Colin ... Renata. Whichever way you coupled them, it came out the same. Was—was Colin's house empty as well?

She would never have known that she asked the question aloud, unless, from the doorway, a voice had not answered her.

'Yes, he's gone, too. Both our birds have flown. But why' ... curiously ... 'did you come to her room, Junia, and not your own? Yet I'm glad you did, it was a quick way of knowing.'

Junia turned and faced Karl Kemble.

'But I don't know,' she appealed, 'I simply ran down the corridor and turned this door handle by mistake. But it wasn't my room, it was Renata's.'

'The room that Renata had. She's left now. The room near the "convenient" steps.'

'Why did you always say that? Why were they convenient? Why would she need those steps?'

'Not for herself, Junia, for Colin. For a quick exit.' Karl Kemble spoke harshly and without any consideration for Junia. Still directly he went on. 'Before you came,' he said, 'it didn't matter. Renata was the only one down at this end of the building. But when someone else arrived it became essential that she have the nearest room to the steps for——' He paused.

'I think you said before for Colin.'

'Yes, I did. You see, Colin used to visit Renata.'

Junia nodded quite unemotionally, and her lack of any emotion surprised yet did not dismay her.

'I knew from the jasmine,' she murmured.

'Jasmine?' Karl looked at her with concern, and she managed a wry smile back; she supposed she must sound disturbed.

'I was aware of it, I mean of the jasmine in Colin's unit. There was that insistent sweet air. But he ... Colin ... always said no, it was the smell of the bush.'

'But you' ... and Karl Kemble's voice was reminding, reminding her of nights on the track ... 'knew it was not the bush.'

'Yes. Then I thought he might be using a different cologne, something like that.' Junia shrugged. 'But when I came in just now it struck me at once, that all-pervading jasmine. I—I couldn't get away from it, it seemed to entrap me.' She paused. 'I knew at last that it was Renata's jasmine, and then I thought: If this room is bare, another room can be bare, too.'

'Making two rooms, two people. You were right, they've gone.'

'Gone?' she echoed.

'That's what I said. I discovered it earlier, so my shock is over now. But you still have yours to face.'

A moment went by. Then:

'You don't seem distressed about it, Karl,' Junia said wonderingly. 'You say your shock is over already—and yet Renata was your fiancée.'

'Was she?' Karl Kemble asked. He came right into the room.

'She had your ring, a lovely ring.'

'I can explain that, if not what came afterwards. Renata had arrived here in answer to my Sydney advertisement for a secretary. My agent down there had inserted the ad and accepted Miss French on my behalf. When she came she seemed efficient and pleasant and I believed I was doing the right thing later in taking her round to give her a general idea of where she was.'

'As you did with me.'

He shrugged that off and continued: 'When she expressed a wish to be taken to an opal mine, I agreed, of course, and we put down at a place some hundred kilometres south from here. She saw the ring. She liked it, so—well——'

'You bought it?'

'Yes. After all, you have to give something back to keep a secretary in a remote place like this. But by heaven, Junia, that was all I did. I don't know at what juncture the ring became something more than a gift, I only know that somewhere, some time, I became an engaged man.' His lips thinned.

'You could have stopped it,' she pointed out.

He shrugged. 'There's still an old-fashioned thing called chivalry.'

'Even in you?'

'In me.'

'But surely you wouldn't have let chivalry take you into a marriage that you didn't want?'

'No, I wouldn't have gone that far, but I couldn't do it at once, the breaking-off, I mean, and when I might have done it, it was—well, wiser that I didn't.'

'You talk in riddles,' she said, perplexed.

'Then let me put it more simply. Your fiancé meanwhile had ensconced himself. Who sent him, whom he was being paid by, whom he was working for, I have yet to find out.'

Junia did not comment on that, instead she asked: 'What did you mean just now when you said it was wiser to act when Colin arrived?'

'Because something began happening in the project, something very grave. We found there was a leak.'

'A leak?'

'Information was getting out. Not just bits and pieces and surmises and anticipations like all camps suffer, unhappily, but—big stuff.'

'But why did you include Colin?' she asked.

'Because it never happened until he came.'

'It could still have been one of your men.'

'We are co-operative. We are one. For a man to cheat here would be to cheat himself.'

'But Colin didn't even work at the project, he had no contact, so nothing to sell, nothing to divulge, nothing to pass on.'

'No, and that made it all the more obvious.' As Junia stared at him incredulously, Karl said: 'All the more obvious that someone was supplying him. Oh, she was very cunning, was Renata, the hand of friendship that she *publicly* extended to Brent was always very restrained, apparently out of pity only, feminine sympathy, merely offered politely since the rest of us had stood coolly aloof from a stranger come only to write a book.' A wry laugh.

'Do—do you think they knew each other before?' asked Junia. 'In Sydney perhaps? Do you think it was all planned?'

Karl shrugged. 'The only thing I know is that quite soon the plan took more manoeuvring than Renata was capable of. For all her slyness, her adroit and practised slyness, she began to be noticed. They were noticed.'

'Noticed?'

'Secret visits on both sides that were not secret. That's why you were aware of jasmine in a man's room, Junia. She was always down there, ostensibly, if asked, to look at a manuscript, but really to check a page of——'

'A page of ciphers,' recalled Junia.

'Yes. She believed she was being secret, but' ... a shrug ... 'she was seen. And that, too, is why Renata needed an exit for Colin after he had visited her of nights.'

'The convenient steps?'

'Yes. The main entrance would have been too obvious.'

'Colin came for information?'

'You're catching on,' he said dryly. 'There had to be information for Colin to prepare and then submit to whatever agency he had signed himself into, gen to be sifted for its value and his ... Brent's ... subsequent reward.'

'It's horrible!' Junia sighed.

'It's one of the unfortunate facts of holes in the ground,' Karl shrugged.

'Colin was a spy.'

'They were both spies.'

'And there was really no book? No column for a mining magazine?'

'No book. No column.'

'And Renata went to Colin and Colin went to Renata only for that?'

Now there was a silence. It grew to a long one.

'Will you answer me, Karl?' asked Junia.

'You're a woman. Find your own answer.'

She thought it over for several minutes.

'It's harder for me,' she told him miserably at length, 'much harder than for you. You see, Karl, unlike Renata I didn't receive a ring on false pretences, I received it in love. Yes, I loved Colin. Well, I loved him once.'

'And now?'

'No, I don't love him now. But it's not because of Renata, it's because——'

'Yes, Junia?'

'It's because it wasn't the same any more,' Junia said in a low voice. 'Never the same when I came here.'

'I think you mean after the journey across?'

'I mean——' But Junia could not finish it. Not then. He had come further up to her now, but they still stood apart.

'Peter?' Karl questioned her next.

'Peter loved me, and I told him that I loved him. I believe I did too. I believe you do love the Peters in life.' Junia paused. 'Are you angry about Peter?'

'You mean for loving you?'

'No, for telling me.'

'Telling you?' he questioned.

'Telling me what he did. You remember, the cardinal rule.'

'What, Junia?'

'You never tell things in a mining project.'

'Quite true, but good lord, that boy, barely any longer here than you, Junia, barely any older, could have told you nothing. You see, we told him nothing. We were trying him out first.'

'Trying him out?' she queried.

'For integrity. Like it or not you have to do that when there's more than one standing to lose. It's distasteful, especially with the Peters who come here, but it still has to be done. Yet I feel certain we need not have concerned ourselves. He could have come through with flying colours.'

'... Yet he did tell me about the gold,' said Junia.

'Gold?'

184

'The message that even a leaf will gossip about. Peter said that to me out at Mary Miranda. He said——'

'Then he was drunk,' interrupted Karl with a smile, 'gold drunk. I've been the same myself when the sun hits those rocks.'

'Then I,' continued Junia, not listening to him, 'told Renata.'

'Yes, I know, and I would beat you soundly for that, except——'

'Except?'

'Except it wasn't and isn't gold. Good lord, we're not interested in gold, not out here.'

'Gold is interesting anywhere,' Junia said dryly.

'But it doesn't turn the wheels of what we want turned. It doesn't build what we want built. Never gold. But don't look intrigued, Miss West, for I'm not telling *you*, because' ... a shrug ... 'you'd only get it wrong again.' Now he was grinning at her.

'Yet who am I to fret over your naïveté?' he continued with laughter, 'for believe me, there can't be anyone more naïve in the world than you. Renata and Colin must have thanked their lucky stars when you arrived here and not anyone else. Anyone else would have had suspicion and doubts, not credulity, faith and trust.' He had said that another time, Junia recalled.

'Yes, who am I to worry, Junia, with the results you got.'

'Results?' she questioned.

'They're gone. *Gone.* Something I wanted very much yet didn't know how to achieve. Oh, I could have sent them away, I suppose, but not so definitely, so inevitably, as you have done.'

'I?'

'Yes, you. You told them there was gold.'

'Well?'

'There was no gold—I just said so. A rumour ... some exaggerated mention of an old prospector with a dolly pot ... a lot of imagination and the sun on the rocks at Mary Miranda ... *but no gold*.'

'And they ... Colin and Renata ... believed——'

'Yes, they believed. More than that they acted, not just sent the usual coded message. "After all," they must have gloated to each other, "gold calls for *negotiations*, for a *personal* approach".'

'Oh, dear!' Junia stood very still for a long moment, and then, compulsively, irresistibly, helplessly, she began to laugh.

Karl stood seriously beside her, then he began to laugh as well.

'They're gone, Junia, gone out of our lives. Gone to some mercenary wretch with a mercenary cheat's false story. They'll never be forgiven by him, they'll be blackballed by similar coteries ... well, I couldn't care less about that ... but they'll also never face up here again, and for that I *do* care.' He grinned.

He became quiet again. Now his face had saddened.

'But someone else has gone out of our lives, too. Peter has.'

'Dear Peter!' sighed Junia.

'Dear Peter,' Karl confirmed, and he came closer still to Junia. He touched her hand gently.

'Yes, they've gone, but you and I remain. "Salute Andronicus and Junia, my kinsmen and fellow-prisoners."' He finished as he had that other time: '*Romans*, 16, 7.'

'But I would never be a prisoner here,' Junia told him eagerly.

'No, you love it,' he nodded. 'I saw that from the first time I met you, I saw you loved my red land, too. I think I loved you then ... I knew I loved you when I saw my morning star.'

186

'But that was weeks after,' she said.

'You're wrong, it happened in the bush coming here.'

'We never saw the star then.'

'You didn't. I did. You see, the star was you. Credulity, faith and trust,' he said again.

'And naïveté?' Junia asked a little shakily; things, she thought, were still going too fast, she felt she couldn't keep up.

'You'll grow out of that, and even if you don't I rather like it, little star, and it doesn't matter. The others do.

'Oh, Junia, Junia, I'm not going to hurry you, I mustn't hurry you—after all, you've only just fallen out of love.'

'But I don't think I have, not really. I don't think I ever was in love, Karl, I think I just liked the idea.'

'Then like this idea, too, girl: In spite of what I said just now, *do* hurry after all, because——'

'Because?' she prompted him.

'Because' ... he searched for words for a moment, then looked at her in triumph ... 'because I say so.' He challenged: 'Remember that?' He had come close up to her now, and both his arms had slipped around her. She made a movement to resist, but could not resist, yet did she want to resist?

'Because' ... and he thought another moment, then grinned. 'Because I'll make you more sorry for yourself than you are now if you don't. Remember when I said both those things to you?'

'I remember a lot of things you said to me. But, Karl, I'm *not* sorry for myself now.'

'If you're not sorry you must be glad.'

'... Perhaps I am glad.'

'But you must make up your mind, mustn't you? No

perhaps. No unsureness. You have to be certain, and you have to stay that way for ever and ever, or else——'

'Or else?' she dared suddenly, running with the fast wind now.

He did not have to search this time for an answer, he warned at once: 'Woman, don't go too far.'

She looked boldly back at him, very sure of herself, enjoying the moment, loving the speed that was racing her to the man she loved ... yes, loved.

'Is that a promise or a threat, Big Brother?' she baited.

'I'm not Big Brother, not to anyone here, and most of all never, and not ever, then, now and in the future ... are you listening to me, Junia West? ... to you.'

He had her in his arms, and his deliberate kiss seemed to fire through her veins. She stood quite still a moment, savouring the sweet capitulation that was trembling through her. Waiting for it. Yearning for her response at last to break through.

Then, unable to postpone the moment any longer, Junia, fellow-prisoner to everything that this man was willing captive, looked up and said warmly and on her own account:

'Not a promise, not a threat, but——'

She returned his long deep kiss.

Did you miss any of these exciting Harlequin Omnibus 3-in-1 volumes?

Anne Hampson #3
Heaven Is High (#1570)
Gold Is the Sunrise (#1595)
There Came a Tyrant (#1622)

Essie Summers #6
The House on Gregor's Brae (#1535)
South Island Stowaway (#1564)
A Touch of Magic (#1702)

Margaret Way

Margaret Way #2
Summer Magic (#1571)
Ring of Jade (#1603)
Noonfire (#1687)

Margaret Malcolm

Margaret Malcolm #2
Marriage by Agreement (#1635)
The Faithful Rebel (#1664)
Sunshine on the Mountains (#1699)

Eleanor Farnes

Eleanor Farnes #2
A Castle in Spain (#1584)
The Valley of the Eagles (#1639)
A Serpent in Eden (#1662)

Kay Thorpe

Kay Thorpe
Curtain Call (#1504)
Sawdust Season (#1583)
Olive Island (#1661)

18 magnificent Omnibus volumes to choose from:

Betty Neels #3
Tangled Autumn (#1569)
Wish with the Candles (#1593)
Victory for Victoria (#1625)

Violet Winspear

Violet Winspear #5
Raintree Valley (#1555)
Black Douglas (#1580)
The Pagan Island (#1616)

Anne Hampson

Anne Hampson #4
Isle of the Rainbows (#1646)
The Rebel Bride (#1672)
The Plantation Boss (#1678)

Margery Hilton

Margery Hilton
The Whispering Grove (#1501)
Dear Conquistador (#1610)
Frail Sanctuary (#1670)

Rachel Lindsay

Rachel Lindsay
Love and Lucy Granger (#1614)
Moonlight and Magic (#1648)
A Question of Marriage (#1667)

Jane Arbor

Jane Arbor #2
The Feathered Shaft (#1443)
Wildfire Quest (#1582)
The Flower on the Rock (#1665)

Great value in reading at $2.25 per volume

Joyce Dingwell #3
Red Ginger Blossom (#1633)
Wife to Sim (#1657)
The Pool of Pink Lilies (#1688)

Hilary Wilde
The Golden Maze (#1624)
The Fire of Life (#1642)
The Impossible Dream (#1685)

Flora Kidd
If Love Be Love (#1640)
The Cave of the White Rose (#1663)
The Taming of Lisa (#1684)

Lucy Gillen #2
Sweet Kate (#1649)
A Time Remembered (#1669)
Dangerous Stranger (#1683)

Gloria Bevan
Beyond the Ranges (#1459)
Vineyard in a Valley (#1608)
The Frost and the Fire (#1682)

Jane Donnelly
The Mill in the Meadow (#1592)
A Stranger Came (#1660)
The Long Shadow (#1681)

Complete and mail this coupon today!